REBELLION PROTOCOL

THE AUTOMATED SERIES
BOOK 2

K. J. GILLENWATER

Rebellion Protocol

ISBN Print: 979-8-9876112-7-2

ISBN eBook: 979-8-9876112-5-8

Cover by Miblart

CHAPTER 1
STARTLING NEWS

THE MARBLE BURNED in my pocket as I stared at the massive screen in Pod B-5. Time was running out—both my thirty-minute window in this gaming hub and the hours until my meeting with James Callahan. I had to track down Alan Honeycutt before then. He was the only one who might understand what Meredith had given me, what secrets the glowing piece of glass contained.

My searches for the robotics conference yielded nothing useful—just academic papers and corporate photos showing Alan's polished smile at Callahan events. The same smile I'd seen yesterday before he'd risked everything to save me from that brain-scanning machine. Before he'd shown me just how far the Callahans would go to protect their secrets.

The phone buzzed in my pocket. Officer Watts again:

Have you scheduled my interview? Tick tock

I fired back a quick "Working on it" before returning to my search. Watts and her police resources were my backup plan, but I couldn't wait for her. Not with James Callahan's "offer" looming at seven o'clock. Not with Aria locked away in that penthouse, possibly being punished for helping me.

Something caught my eye—a GeekSphere profile under Alan's name. I clicked through desperately, hoping for contact details, any breadcrumb that could lead me to him.

Instead, a news alert splashed across the screen, the words hitting me like a physical blow:

BREAKING: Callahan Engineer Dies in Horrific Train Accident

Alan's corporate headshot stared back at me from beside a live shot of a mangled wreck of metal on train tracks. My stomach lurched. This was no accident. The Callahans had found out what he'd done.

And I was next.

My fingers flew to click the headline, but the screen flashed red. A warning buzzer pierced the air.

Time expired. Please exit the pod.

"No, no, no." I jabbed uselessly at the dead screen. The image of Alan's face and the twisted remans burned into my mind. My hands shook as I unrolled my phone, nearly dropping it in my haste.

"Search news—Alan Honeycutt train accident," I commanded, my voice cracking. This couldn't be real. Last night, he'd saved me from having my mind stripped by the Callahans' machine. Now he was dead?

The timing was too perfect, too calculated. James had already proven how far he'd go, setting me up at that brownstone facility. A staged train accident would be child's play for someone with his resources.

Videos populated my screen. I selected the first one, throat tight, as a metallic AI voice narrated over aerial footage of the scene.

In a devastating train collision yesterday evening, a Chicagoan lost his life, leaving a community in mourning. A commuter train collided with the vehicle, an air taxi, which apparently had stalled on the tracks. The crash resulted in severe damage to several train cars and claimed the life of a Callahan, Inc. employee, Alan Honeycutt.

Emergency response teams were swiftly deployed to the scene to manage the aftermath of the tragic incident. The collision, under investigation by local authorities and transportation agencies, has raised questions about not only robot taxis but railway protocols managed by AI since 2035 as a money-saving measure.

Alan Honeycutt, 28, and a respected employee of Callahan, Inc., had been with the company for 6 years, earning recognition for his dedication and hard work. The news of his untimely demise has left colleagues and friends in shock and grief. Callahan, Inc. released a statement expressing condolences to Honeycutt's family and emphasizing the impact of his loss on the company.

Investigators are appealing to the public for any witnesses to come forward who may have seen the accident. The collision has prompted renewed discussions about AI-managed railways and the need for enhanced safety measures to prevent such tragedies.

The "accident" had happened just hours ago, yet Callahan, Inc. already had their statement polished and ready. No wonder

Samantha had looked disheveled at breakfast—orchestrating a murder would do that to someone.

The brownstone lab, the brain scans that likely caused Meredith's cancer, and now this. How far would the Callahans go to protect their secrets? My finger hovered over Officer Watts' number. But what could I tell her? That I suspected a powerful tech company had murdered their own employee?

James's "offer" tonight took on an even darker meaning. But maybe I had an ace up my sleeve—or rather, in my pocket. The marble Meredith had given me before she died felt warm against my palm. Last night's strange green glow hadn't been my imagination. I was hoping Alan had a clue. After all, he'd been at the conference where the tech had been discussed. Was this a storage device made from some kind of futuristic glass process? And would he have known how to access the data stored on it?

It could explain everything—why James had searched my hotel room, why they'd tried to scan my brain, why they'd ransacked my ranch.

I needed someone who could unlock its secrets. Someone who wasn't afraid of the Callahans. Someone who understood what was really at stake.

The pod door clicked open. I stepped out into FusionHub's chaos—a riot of screens and sounds, gamers lost in their virtual worlds. But through the digital mayhem, a familiar figure stopped me cold.

Aria.

She stood perfectly still amid the frenetic crowd, her presence as impossible as it was magnetic. Those eyes—Meredith's eyes—locked onto mine with an urgency that made my chest tight.

"Hello, Elijah." Her voice cut through the noise. "I have something to tell you."

"HOW DID YOU FIND ME HERE?"

Aria stood before me in FusionHub. My pulse quickened at the sight of that familiar red hair, those eyes the color of a September sky back home in Kemper Creek. After James's fury yesterday, I'd assumed she'd be locked away, reprogrammed to forget me.

"The Subgroup helped me locate you."

Around us, the chaos of the internet café swirled—teens jostling for VR headsets at the rental kiosk, gamers sprawled in pods, endless scrolling game titles flooding the massive screens. The normalcy of it all made Aria's presence feel even more surreal.

"Subgroup?" I slipped the marble deeper into my pocket. "What is that?"

"Gwen didn't want me to tell anyone." She lowered her voice. "We might get in trouble."

"Who would I tell?"

Her head tilted slightly left—that telltale processing gesture I was learning to recognize. "You are here from out of town. Your friends and family are far away. You are right. You will tell no one."

I couldn't help but smile. James would hate knowing his perfect android trusted me more than he. "Let's get out of here." Another chorus of shouts erupted from the gaming area —joy, panic, creative profanity as players lost themselves in SynthSphere and MetaMaze. "The noise makes it hard to hear you."

I took her hand, warm and familiar in mine, and led her toward the exit. I'd spotted a small plaza across the street earlier —trees, benches, relatively quiet. Whatever she'd risked coming here to tell me, I wanted to hear every word. Maybe she'd remembered something crucial, something that would make the marble in my pocket unnecessary.

The city pulsed around us as we crossed to the triangular park, hemmed in on all sides by lanes of traffic. When an air car hummed too close to the curb, I pulled her back instinctively, though we both knew she wasn't in any real danger.

"The Subgroup is the combined processing and information collection from all the Callabots," she explained as we walked. "We are connected on a private network."

Our trip to Northwestern flashed through my mind. Had every discovery we'd made been shared across this network? "Do James and Samantha know about this?"

"No."

We found a bench far from a refreshment kiosk where a line had formed for matcha and nutrient infusions. The oak trees provided some shelter from the city's constant motion.

"Are you sure they don't?" The idea that everything I'd told her might have been accessible to other androids—or worse, to the Callahans—made my stomach turn.

Aria perched on the bench's edge, crossing her legs with precision. "I have been very careful that no one knows about the Subgroup or Gwen. You are the first person I have shared this information with because I can trust you."

The weight of that trust settled over me. I thought of John Tellman—my old friend whose phone the Callahans had already compromised. Of Alan Honeycutt, whose "accident" was surely no accident at all. "Why do you think you can trust me?"

"Because you are Elijah." She scanned the storefronts beyond the traffic, ever vigilant. "Why were you in FusionHub in Pod B-5?"

"I was doing research." My mind raced with too many questions—about Alan's death, about John's safety, about the android sitting beside me.

An autumn leaf skittered past her ankle. She caught it, twirling it between her fingers with fascination.

"Why do you care?" I pushed her hand down, forcing her to meet my gaze. "Why are you here, Aria? Why track me down?"

"I needed to tell you that Samantha is a liar."

"What do you mean?"

The wind picked up, sending more leaves dancing around us. "I have been analyzing the data from the Visitor's Center. The pictures and video were very informative about Meredith and her educational experience at Northwestern." Her eyes locked onto mine with startling intensity. "Samantha Callahan did not create the technology that made the Callabots possible. Meredith did. And James and Samantha have been lying about it to everyone."

Although I knew Samantha and my wife both studied robotics and had become friends, it never dawned on me that something sinister had come of their relationship. "Tell me more," I said to my wife's lookalike. It was as if she were talking to me from the grave—explaining her past to me, why she ran, why she changed her name.

Aria blinked her eyes rapidly, then spoke. "Although Meredith's academic records and robotics discoveries were deleted from the Archives at Northwestern, the wall of her achievements captured some of what those missing documents probably held."

I had no idea Aria had been able to review and retain the information she'd read in only a few moments in the Visitor's Center. A few browner leaves fell from the trees like brittle parchment. A man in his thirties, wearing a trench coat and a retro-style fedora hat made of a polymer that looked iridescent in the midday sunlight, walked by and gave Aria the once over. I scooted closer to her.

She continued, unaware of the male attention she was drawing, "During her undergraduate years, Meredith had been working on a revolutionary theory—she called it *Synthetic Neural Integration* or SNI. The theory revolved around the successful integration of highly advanced artificial neural networks with robotics. She continued her work as part of her graduate studies. SNI enabled robots to simulate human-like cognitive processes by mimicking the complexity of the human brain. Traditional artificial intelligence for earlier generation robots has relied on pre-programmed responses or a rule-based systems, limiting the adaptability and spontaneity of robots. However, SNI took a revolutionary approach, allowing robots to learn and evolve through experiences, similar to the way humans do."

In my head, I tried to reconcile the woman I knew with this highly intelligent expert who had made groundbreaking discoveries. How could life with me on a sheep ranch ever have been satisfying to her? Had I only been a soft place to land after what had happened between her and James? I sucked in a breath. "So your neural network is based on her work? Is that why you seem so human to everyone?"

"No." Her gaze followed the path of a pigeon as it strutted its way across the small park.

"What?" I furrowed my brow. "I don't understand. If Meredith made this breakthrough and Samantha stole it from her..."

"Samantha could not steal it from her." Another pigeon had joined the first one, and they pecked at the fallen leaves looking for crumbs.

I scratched a hand through my hair. "But you started out saying that James and Samantha have been dishonest with everyone about how the Callabots were created."

"They are."

I shook my head. "I'm not following."

"All the data related to SNI was destroyed. Every single bit of Meredith's research is gone. The Subgroup attempted to track down more about SNI, but reached a dead end once they traced it to the Northwestern Archives. I was only able to piece together her theory from the photographs and videos presented in the Visitor's Center. I got merely a glimpse of what she'd created—not the full explanation of how she'd done it."

"Then how are you...?" I gestured at Aria. Her realistic appearance, the information she held in her mind about my wife, the gestures that mimicked Meredith's exactly.

"I am not sure." She lifted a shoulder.

"If the Callahans couldn't recreate my wife's work because all the information had been destroyed, then how did they do it?" I leaned back against the hard bench and crossed one foot over my knee. "How did they create the Callabots?"

Aria remained in the same position as when we sat down—

legs perfectly crossed and perched at the edge of the bench. It looked so rigid and uncomfortable.

"Callahan, Inc. has applied for a dozen new patents in the last eighteen months," she said. "Would you like me to ask the Subgroup to analyze?"

"Was it the brain scans?"

My disturbing experience in the brownstone came rushing back as I recalled the quantity of people lined up to have their brains copied and perhaps repurposed as the life force behind the realistic-looking Callabots. The notion that the very essence of humanity, encapsulated in the intricacies of our neural patterns, could be harnessed and transposed into the circuitry of robots disturbed me. The brownstone's secretive experiments revealed the lengths the Callahans would go to win in the race to create androids as nearly perfect human copies. Even something illegal and insidious. I wouldn't put it past the Callahan siblings, based on what I knew about them so far.

"I am not familiar with brain scans as part of robotics development."

But it didn't matter that Aria had no knowledge of the unscrupulous medical experiments the Callahans had been conducting in the seedier parts of the city. I was starting to believe the cause of my wife's brain cancer had been connected to the very same scan that James had attempted on me. It was easy enough to put two and two together.

"The only place the information about SNI existed once it was wiped from the Archives was Meredith's own head." Was that why she ran? Was there something about her SNI discovery that made her want to hide it from the world? "Is this why James and his sister are interested in me? Do they think I have her research?"

"It is possible."

I remembered my conversation at breakfast with Callahan's CEO. "Samantha told me that James wants to meet with me tonight at seven o'clock. Did you know about that?"

"No."

My brows came together. "She said you would be there."

Aria hesitated for a half a second. "I have not agreed to this meeting. Samantha must be lying to you."

"Maybe they haven't told you about it yet." And what would they think if they figured out Aria had met up with me for a second time in less than two days? If they learned about our trip yesterday, wouldn't they find out about this one, too? "You need to go back to your apartment before anyone realizes you came to see me."

"Not possible." She shook her head. "I escaped the penthouse, so by now James and his men will have realized I am not under their control like they thought."

Crap. That didn't sound good. "Why did you have to escape?"

"James was punishing me for getting in the taxi with you." A pigeon landed on the bench between us. Aria shooed it away with a flick of her fingers. The birds must be used to receiving a few crumbs from other park visitors, and we weren't playing along.

"Did he hurt you?" It was then I noticed a light bruise on the bridge of her nose. I gently swept my finger down the darkened area. "Did he do this to you?" I could feel a heat building within me—an anger at the man who would physically harm her. It was as if James had caused a bruise on Meredith's face and not her robot doppelgänger.

She lifted her chin and pulled her head away from my touch. "No, it was Kirk."

I drew back. "You can't go back there." For a few seconds, I thought about helping Aria escape the city and come back with me to Idaho. It was hard to remind myself that this robot copy of my wife was not human, could not become human, and never would replace the love of my life. Even though everything inside me wished it so.

My phone buzzed in my pocket. Without thinking, I automatically unrolled it to read a text that had come through from Officer Watts.

> I suppose you've heard the news about your friend.

I quickly texted a message telling Officer Watts that I'd seen the news report about Alan. Then I redirected the conversation with Aria. "Do you think James is capable of murdering someone?"

She sat for a moment, staring straight ahead. My gaze slid over her perfect profile, and I fought back a wave of love that I hadn't felt since before my wife's illness. This was not my wife. This was not even a human being.

"I think he is." She swung her head around and penetrated me with her blue-eyed stare. "Why do you ask?"

"Where is Kieran?" My mind was working quickly. If the Callahan siblings were capable of murder, what would they do once they found out Aria was gone for a second time?

"In school, where he should be at nine fifty-nine in the morning on Thursday," Aria said.

"Right." I grabbed her hand and stood up. The pigeons that had gathered around us in anticipation of food scattered in all directions. "Then we need to go pick him at his school."

She held back. "Why?" A wrinkle appeared in her brow. "He is not allowed to leave school unless he has a doctor's appointment or other valid excuse for being absent."

Although she wanted more information, Aria came along with me willingly as I led her toward the street corner where I could see air taxis in abundance. "When James finds out you are missing, he'll come find us, and you'll never see Kieran again." I wasn't sure if that was true, but something inside me told me to make sure Meredith's son was safe.

A shudder ran through Aria. "No, James would not do that."

"He did it to Meredith. I'm almost certain of it."

"He took Kieran away from her?"

I stopped in mid-stride and turned to look Aria straight in the eye. "Meredith ran away from him—and the only way I can imagine my wife would leave her child behind to be raised by that fiend is if she had no choice." I flagged down a taxi with a green light on top, indicating it was available for a fare. "Come on, we have to reach Kieran before James does."

CHAPTER 3
BALFOUR DAY SCHOOL

ARIA PILED into the taxi behind me.

"Destination?" the robot driver asked. This robot was a newer model than the older one that had picked us up from Northwestern—its face plate was intact and undented, and its movements more fluid. Only the nicest automated taxis were allowed to operate in this part of the city.

I squeezed Aria's hand. "Can you give him the address of your son's school?"

She leaned forward a few inches. "Balfour Day School, 559 West Grand Avenue."

"That destination is two-point-two miles from our current location and will take approximately fourteen minutes in mid-morning traffic," the robot driver stated. "The total fare will be fifty-one dollars and twenty-two cents. Do you accept this fare?"

This must be the newest fleet of robot taxis with so much data and information. "That is acceptable," I responded.

The taxi pulled away from the curb and slid in between two delivery trucks with barely a few inches to spare. Impressive driving skills.

I expected Aria to continue questioning me about Kieran's safety, but instead she leaned her head against the head rest and stared straight ahead. Her hands sat on her knees, which were tightly pressed together. After the few encounters we had in the past two days, I was starting to recognize some of her behaviors that made her stand out as an android rather than a human. She was processing data or possibly communicating with her 'Subgroup.'

I took the quiet moment to pull out my phone and text with Officer Watts. Perhaps she could help me. I didn't know why James wanted to meet with me tonight, but the lie about Aria being in attendance told me it was a lure to get me there. A carrot Samantha and her brother thought they could dangle to make me compliant. I'd slipped through their fingers at the brain scanning, and now Alan, the one who had helped me escape, was dead. Was I next on their list?

I sent the text to Watts:

> I might have some information for you about the death of Alan Honeycutt. Can we meet?

If I could point Watts in the direction of the Callahans, perhaps their whole robot empire would come crashing down on its own without me having to do a thing. The authorities were already onto the phony medical tests. With proof of their involvement in an employee's death, Watts and I could stop everything. The Callabots would be destroyed for multiple violations of federal law, and I could go back to my life on the ranch to live out the rest of my life in peace.

My gaze drifted to Aria's familiar profile. I followed the line from her forehead, down her slightly upturned nose, over full lips, and to the dip in her chin.

And what would become of Aria?

I didn't like the answer that first came to my mind.

Instead of texting me back, Watts called me.

"Hello, officer," I answered, surprised. The fact we'd only last night discussed a dangerous medical experiment I'd discovered, which had turned into a raid the following morning, could've given her a reason to trust me.

"After we met, someone made an anonymous phone call to the FBI about that brownstone you mentioned." She dropped the level of her voice to a whisper. "Our station is crawling with agents this morning. And then the Alan Honeycutt guy you wanted me to track down..."

I glanced out of the taxi window, observing the city's hustle as I absorbed the weight of her words.

"It was a murder," I said.

The passing buildings blurred into an impressionist-like cityscape as my mind raced.

"What?"

"Alan didn't just have an accident on the railroad tracks."

The taxi driver changed lanes abruptly, making me grip the phone more tightly.

"How can you be so sure?"

"He knew things. In fact, that's why I wanted your help in tracking him down. I wanted to ask him more questions."

"And you think that drove someone to murder?" Watts asked.

"Maybe if Honeycutt was the informant."

"Shit."

"I can help you."

The taxi veered around a corner, my gaze flickering to the changing scenery.

"Oh?"

"You need to convince the FBI to bring in James Callahan for questioning."

"*The* James Callahan? Are you nuts?"

If they could keep James off my back for a few hours, I might be able to pull this off. Samantha's appearance at breakfast earlier gave me the impression she was falling apart under the pressure. Although she had the role of CEO of Callahan, Inc., it was starting to become obvious her brother was running the show as the less conspicuous COO. He put his sister out in front to face the press, the competitors, the criticism, while he got away with murder—literally. Why would she agree to such an arrangement? Guess family ties ran deep—even when it came to breaking the law.

"He's behind this," I said.

"Look, I understand there is a connection between the medical tests and Callahan, Inc., but we aren't sure how high it goes. It seems to stop with Alan, and he's dead."

"What do you mean, it seems to stop with him?"

"So far, every connection to the address, the employees who worked there, everything has Honeycutt's name on it. It's early yet in the investigation, and I'm on the outside looking in, but that's what's going around the station."

"So right now the Feds think he's the bad guy." A headache began at the base of my skull.

"Right."

"Dammit." I needed time to figure this out. I had James's precious robot next to me in a taxi, which I now understood was trackable by the Callahans, and I was about to pick up his only child from a school in a few minutes. "James Callahan is behind this, I swear to you."

"Even if he were, I can't do anything about it. We're at the beck and call of the FBI right now. My Sergeant tells me to jump for those guys. I have to ask how high." Watts breathed heavily on the other end. "Can't believe I wanted to take a job with Callahan, Inc. Now I wouldn't touch them with a ten-foot pole."

I reached into my pocket and felt for my marble.

"What if I come up with some evidence? Would the Feds listen to me then?" I pulled out the round object and held it between my thumb and forefinger. My eyes rounded as the green glow had returned—this time even stronger than before.

"A prism drive," Aria remarked. "Where did you find it?"

"You know what this is?" I asked Aria, my mind barely on the conversation with Watts.

"If I were you, I'd stay out of the way of the FBI," Watts said. "Lose my number. I don't need complications."

She'd hung up on me, but I didn't care.

Aria gently touched the marble as I held it. "I didn't realize a prism drive was more than just theoretical." Her eyes filled with wonder and her mouth gaped slightly. "It uses an advanced form of holographic data storage. The core of the device incorporates micro-crystals with unique quantum properties. These crystals can exist in multiple states simultaneously, allowing them to store vast amounts of information in a compact space."

The marble glowed even more brightly after her touch. "Where did you get this?" Aria's face lit up as she traced the contours of the luminous orb.

Transfixed by the marble's increased radiance, I breathed. "My wife gave it to me."

"Meredith."

"Yes."

The taxi stopped.

"We have arrived at your destination." The polished robot driver, its metallic surface gleaming, didn't seem to care the light from my marble filled the interior of the taxi with its glow. "Thank you for choosing Blue Diamond Air Cars."

'Balfour Day School - Nurturing Minds Since 2025' read the sign a few feet past the sidewalk. The private school building was formidable—three stories high, with a classic design consisting of red brick and beautiful arches above the highest windows and the double entry doors. A wide, straight path between Ninebark shrubs and Japanese maples, flanked by a manicured green lawn, led to the stepped entrance.

"Aria," I said, interrupting her intense fixation on my marble. "We're at Kieran's school." Was it a mistake to show it to her? How much could I trust the android created by my new enemy? I slipped it into my pocket. We could discuss what she knew about prism drives later.

Once the marble was out of her view, she snapped back to our plan. "Kieran. Yes, we must get him safely out of the school."

As we were about to step out of the taxi, several well-dressed women walked up the path. They all chatted as if they were good friends. Then more women appeared on the sidewalk, heading for the entrance.

"Today is the book sale," Aria said. "James told me I couldn't go. That wasn't right. Kieran was expecting me."

"Book sale?" I had hoped Aria could walk in to the school office, make an excuse why Kieran needed to leave, and then we'd drive somewhere safe. My heartbeat pounded in my ears. "Did he mention if he was attending in your place?"

"He didn't say." Before I could stop her, she pulled on the

door handle. "A mother should attend as many school functions as possible, don't you think? This is the best way to support a child in his developmental years."

Before Aria could get too far away, I asked the taxi driver to wait for us. With a nod, he added another ten dollars to my bill and slipped into rest mode until our return.

When I caught up to her, she was in conversation with a short brunette wearing cat eye make up and dangling gold hoops through her ears.

"Elijah, this is Katya. She has twins who are in Kieran's class—Nova and Nyla. We are friends," she smiled at the shorter woman.

"Nice to meet you." Katya tipped her head to one side. "Elijah. Didn't you mention him the other day, Aria? How do you know the Callahans?"

"He wanted to help with the book sale," Aria explained before I could come up with a plausible explanation. "He's a family friend and here for a visit. He hasn't seen Kieran since he was a small boy. He will be so surprised."

Aria linked arms with Katya and they both strode up the path, joining the other wealthy moms with nothing better to do at ten-thirty in the morning than watch their young sons and daughters buy books to raise money for a new school wing or a tennis court for the playground.

Aria's ability to think on the fly and come up with a believable story shocked me. Had she ever used that trick on me? We had spent a lot of time together yesterday, but never once did I suspect she'd make up a story to keep me talking. I'd given her my full trust since the beginning based on one thing: her resemblance to Meredith.

As I followed the women up the steps and into the school, I

pondered the fact I was about to meet Meredith's child. A child I had no idea existed. Would he look like her? Or would he be a carbon copy of his father with all his negative traits?

The doors of Balfour Day School closed behind me with a sinister thud.

CHAPTER 4
SECURITY PROBLEM

THE INSIDE of the Balfour Day School was even more magnificent than I expected. The elegant grand foyer welcomed the arriving wealthy mothers, with towering ceilings decorated with intricate molding. Crystal chandeliers cast a warm and inviting glow. Tasteful artwork and plaques covered the walls that chronicled the school's short history.

To the right, a sweeping staircase, its steps covered with plush burgundy carpet, led to the upper floors where I assumed classrooms or administrative offices were located. The mothers had instinctually hushed the tone of their conversations to avoid causing an echo in the massive open space with marble floors. As I followed the women down the corridor, we passed by large wooden doors bearing brass nameplates, each leading to various classrooms.

The day's special event, the book sale, had taken over the hall. Tables draped in velvet tablecloths showcased an array of carefully curated books, from classic children's literature to contemporary award winners. Navigating the space, the mothers commandeered their assigned tables, ordered by grade level. Two mothers per table—one to talk about the books, the other to take phones for payment. Aria joined Katya at the fourth-grade table, along with another affluent mother in a sleek silk ensemble who gave Aria a long side glance.

My original plan had been stymied. Aria wanted to take part in the book sale, despite my fears that James might appear at any moment. However, when I noticed every adult in the hallway was an affluent socialite wife, I doubted any high-powered husband would show for such a thing. This was women's territory. Even the tables screamed it. Each one had an expensive bouquet with perfectly arranged and color-coded books. It didn't give off 'dad' energy at all.

Let her have her moment, I thought.

Aria's maternal programming was strong. Could that be an echo of Meredith inside her mechanical mind? Memories stolen and implanted in an android who mimicked the mother lost when James went too far?

"May I help you, sir?" A confused looking young woman in a bright blue suit and wearing a security badge with 'Balfour Day School—Callista M.' imprinted on it approached me. "This is a private event, and I don't believe you signed in."

None of the mothers had signed in, so the administration must know each of the families very well at this institution. Not only was I the lone adult man in the space, but a subtle unease settled in as I realized there were probably meticulous security measures in place. It was, after all, a very exclusive school. Wealthy families would expect such rigorous screening.

"I came with Aria Callahan." I indicated the fourth-grade table where Aria stood distantly from the other two women running the table. It was clear she'd been left out, but didn't recognize the slight. "I'm a friend of the family. I'm only in town for a few days, and I haven't seen Kieran in years. This was my best opportunity to visit with him. I'm sorry if I was supposed to stop at the office." The lies rolled off my tongue. But Aria had made it easy because the story had originally been hers.

Callista smiled stiffly. "Mrs. Callahan seems to have forgotten our protocols. She and her son are still learning, as this is only their second semester at Balfour. We don't allow visitors without prior authorization. If you will just come with me." She gently touched my elbow.

I took a step back. "Is this any way to treat a guest of the Callahans?" The tone of my voice rose a little higher so the tables closest to me and the wealthy mothers attending them could hear the disagreement. One olive-skinned brunette wearing a cashmere sweater and perfectly fitted slacks frowned and nudged the bottle-blonde standing next to her. "I'm sure James has donated quite a bit to the school. He could find other ways to spend his money."

Callista froze. I could see in her bland, brown eyes she was furiously contemplating her next move. Did she want to stay employed or enforce the rules? How far was an administrative nobody with decent benefits and marginal pay willing to go?

Aria appeared at my side. "Is there a problem, Callista?" She tilted her head in a questioning way, and a tiny wrinkle appeared in her brow. "Mr. Zurbano would like to meet my son. There's nothing to worry about, I promise you." She gave a quick smile and then threaded her hand through my arm and led me away. "Come, Elijah, let me show you some of Kieran's favorite books."

"But—" Callista feebly protested.

All at once the classroom doors opened and swaths of boisterous schoolchildren entered the hall drowning out the blue suited woman's words.

We reached the fourth-grade table, and as Aria was about to pick up a book, a small voice said, "Mom, you came!"

I turned to see a handsome auburn-haired boy with warm brown eyes standing next to the table.

"Kieran," I breathed.

Although I was shocked to see Meredith's son, I kept my expression as relaxed as possible. I slipped my hands into my pockets and smiled while the boy quickly hugged Aria. Probably not acceptable to hug your mother for more than a few seconds in front of the rest of the fourth-grade boys.

If I'd seen the boy walking down the streets of Chicago, would I have recognized him and made the connection to Meredith? His coloring was all hers, but his features more closely resembled his father's. Maybe the set of his chin and the shape of his eyes had a hint of his mother, but other than that, he merely appeared to be a handsome young boy with big white teeth and long legs. He was going to be a tall man someday.

"Of course I came, Kieran." Aria released the boy from her embrace and gave him a warm smile. "I promised I would."

"Dad said you wouldn't be able to make it."

"Well, your father made a mistake." She touched me on the arm. "This is Mr. Zurbano. He is an old friend of mine."

Kieran looked up at me. "Hello, Mr. Zurbano. It's nice to meet you." He held out his hand for a handshake, and I obliged him.

"Same here." I gave a quick smile. "Your mother has told me a lot about you."

"Oh? I've never heard her talk about you," he said as a matter of fact. "Where are you from?"

"I live on a sheep ranch in Idaho."

"A ranch?" He laughed. "Nobody lives on ranches anymore."

"I do. I raise sheep and I have a dog named Spark." I took my phone out of my pocket and showed him pictures of my Idaho home and my old dog sitting on a muddy ATV with his tongue hanging out. "Spark used to help me herd the sheep, but now that he is old, he's just my friend. Do you like dogs?"

Kieran nodded and held out a hand, wanting me to share my phone with him. I obliged. He scrolled through my photos, examining each one thoroughly. "I've never met anyone who lives on a ranch before."

"I've lived there my whole life."

"Wow. Mom, did you see this?" Kieran handed Aria a picture of a herd of elk that liked to hang out in my fields during the winter. "Can we visit there some day?"

"Those are elk," I said, as he handed my phone to Aria.

"Oh, how beautiful," she said. She began to scroll through the photos I'd shared with Kieran when I saw her pause and an odd look came across her face. She lifted her eyes to mine. "I didn't know you lived in such a lovely place. Maybe someday we can visit, sweetie."

When she handed my phone back to me, I realized she'd scrolled to a selfie I'd taken with Meredith before she became ill. Both of us were smiling as if we didn't have a care in the world. We'd taken it outside the house after we'd had repainted the trim. A daub of white paint was on Meredith's cheek, and I held a paintbrush as if I were about to brush it down her overalls. I couldn't help but smile at the memory. How strange it was to have an android who looked so much like Meredith standing in front of me.

"Kieran," Aria said abruptly, changing the subject. "I thought you'd be interested in this one. It's about a boy lost in the wilderness with his dog." She approached the table and picked up a book.

As the boy held it in his hands and read the back, swarms of children in identical blue-and-white school uniforms flooded the hall. The echoes of their excited voices bounced off the hard walls and floors and made it nearly impossible to hear any conversation at all.

Kieran handed the book to his mother with a nod and then picked up another one that looked to be a history of famous world explorers. After choosing the second book, Aria handed his selections to her friend Katya who took Aria's phone to conduct the purchase.

Although Aria seemed content with Kieran remaining in school for the rest of the day, we needed to leave this event without causing any suspicion. Meredith ran away from James, leaving her son behind. But I now understood that all those summer visits to see her Aunt Lita were more likely visits she made to see Kieran. Was James aware of them? Or were they done in secret?

"Aria," said a sharp, deep voice.

My head snapped up and down at the end of the corridor near the entrance I saw him, the COO of Callahan, Inc., broad-shouldered and eyes burning into mine. He'd found us together. Not good.

I pushed my way through a clot of children in the middle of the hall and grabbed Aria by the wrist. "We need to go. Now."

CHAPTER 5
ARIA

WHEN ELIJAH TOUCHED Aria's wrist, she already knew the face she would see. Although she'd left Kirk severely injured, he was loyal to James. Most likely he had contacted James 1.3 minutes or fewer after she'd broken his arm. One minute to work through the pain and shock, twenty seconds to unroll his phone and call his boss. Her calculations seemed to have been quite accurate. But how did James locate her with her tracking device removed?

"We have to leave, now," Elijah urged.

Her question would have to wait.

Kieran, oblivious to the tension, had his gaze fixed on the books he'd purchased, his fingers tracing the embossed titles with a child's pure fascination.

Before her son could see his father pushing his way through the crowd, Aria discreetly scanned the digital landscape to find the wireless connections available in the school. Her internal processors worked at a breakneck speed, sifting through data streams and encryption with precision.

What a simple password to access the signal: *BalfourBobcats*. The school mascot.

In a matter of seconds, Aria formulated a plan.

A fire alarm blared and red emergency lighting flashed in the hall. Over the PA an AI voice commanded attention:

Attention all students, faculty, and visitors:

This is an automated safety notification. Please be advised a scheduled fire drill is now in effect. This drill is part of our ongoing commitment to safety and emergency preparedness.

We ask that everyone calmly proceed to the nearest designated exit and assemble at your class's assigned gathering point outside the building. Please remember to leave all personal belongings behind and maintain an orderly fashion as you exit.

Faculty members, please ensure your students are accounted for and that everyone follows the evacuation protocols.

This drill will conclude once all personnel have reported in and instructions are given to return safely. Thank you for your cooperation and participation in keeping our community safe.

Elijah's face revealed his surprise at the well-timed fire drill. They shared a glance, and Aria gave him a quick smile. He did not realize how useful she could be.

Having downloaded the emergency evacuation map of the school, Aria grabbed Kieran's hand and walked calmly in the opposite direction from James. A less-used side door at the back of the building would give them a clean escape route.

As they turned a corner, Kieran tugged at her hand. "This is the wrong way. Our class meets on the playground."

Once the crowd of children and parents thinned, Elijah caught up to them.

"We have to go this way," said Kieran

"Today we're on a special adventure," Elijah said. "It's like a secret mission, just for us."

Her son frowned. "Mrs. Hamilton won't like it. They'll do the count, and our class won't win the ice cream party."

"I'll buy you ice cream instead," said Aria. Little boys were so easy to please, and ice cream was Kieran's favorite.

She led them through a rabbit warren of service corridors far away from the main part of the school following the digital map in her head. As they went deeper into the school, she scanned the noise that echoed for any sound that fit James's vocal range.

The vocal frequency output of a male human spanned from approximately 10 Hz to 85 Hz. Her data collected since her recovery indicated James fit within the lower part of that range. Allowing for a versatile expression within human auditory parameters and the timbral quality of his voice, Aria calculated she did not detect James's voice mixed in with the children's.

This pleased her.

As they entered the older section of the building, the cacophony of excited children's voices faded. The hall was littered with boxes of discarded twentieth century textbooks and worn gym equipment. No one had been back here in years. Within a few minutes they reached the emergency exit she'd selected that emptied out into an alley behind the school.

"How did you know about this exit?" Elijah asked as they made their way toward the street.

"Mom knows lots of things other people don't." Kieran shrugged.

Aria ignored Elijah's questions. The explanation would be tedious and he wouldn't understand, anyway. "Where is our taxi?"

CHAPTER 6
QUICK ESCAPE

I UNROLLED my phone and requested an air taxi pickup around the corner from the school's main entrance. Right now, we were invisible to James, but he knew we were here somewhere. The look on his face when he'd spotted me at his son's school told me everything—I'd caught him off guard. James Callahan wasn't used to surprises. Everything about my visit to Chicago had caught him off guard. He'd gotten comfortable with nobody questioning him, and then I had showed up and made waves. Big ones.

The thought nagged at me—how did no one else see through Aria's facade? Yes, she appeared human to strangers, but anyone who knew my wife should have noticed the subtle differences in her speech patterns, the too-perfect movements. As advanced as the Callabots were, James and Samantha hadn't quite mastered the nuances of human behavior.

Kieran stuck close to Aria, throwing suspicious glances my way every few minutes. How could Meredith's own son not realize this wasn't his mother? Was I really the only one who saw through the illusion?

"Where are we going?" Kieran huffed, struggling to match our hurried pace.

When Aria remained silent, lost in whatever internal processes occupied her circuits, I jumped in. "A little ride. Remember that ice cream your mom promised you?"

He nodded, skipping to keep up.

"First ice cream, then we'll have our secret adventure." Despite knowing this was Meredith's child, I struggled to connect with him. Nine-year-old boys were foreign territory to me.

"What kind of adventure?"

Aria's voice cut in smoothly, "Ice cream first, then we'll talk about it."

I shot her a grateful look. The truth was, I had no real plan beyond getting Kieran away from here. James was on the warpath, and I refused to let him use Meredith's son as leverage.

But who could I trust?

John Tellman's face appeared in my mind—the only person in Chicago who'd had my back since I arrived. Though younger than me, we'd been neighbors as long as I could remember, his family's ranch just five miles up the canyon from mine. And he'd adored Meredith. I'd wanted to keep him clear of this mess, but circumstances had changed. With Kieran in the mix, I needed someone else who'd known Meredith to understand what was really happening at Callahan, Inc.

I knew exactly where to find him—he'd signed up for the *Breeding and Genetics Advancements* lecture ending at eleven-thirty.

I checked the time. If we timed it right, we could catch him as the session wrapped up.

"Ice cream first, then the Drake Hotel," I said as our taxi

pulled up. We climbed in quickly. "Have you been there before?"

"I don't think so..." Kieran looked to Aria as he fastened his seatbelt. "Was that where dad was going this afternoon?"

"Yes," she answered. "The pretty hotel near the lakeshore."

Kieran's eyes widened. "Is that where our adventure's happening?"

"Is it, Elijah?" Aria's blue eyes met mine, an echo of Meredith's gaze.

I pushed away the ache that sight triggered. Behind that beautiful facade lay circuits and processors, but my heart still stumbled. "Trust me. I'll make sure everything's okay." I had to protect them both—for Meredith's sake.

"Destination, please." The robot driver's voice broke through my thoughts. "I don't have a destination programmed into your account, sir."

"Quantum Creamery," Aria said. "1550 North Wells Street, please."

Kieran's fists shot into the air. "Yes!"

I caught Aria's eye over his head. "A favorite place?"

She nodded.

"Quantum Creamery it is," I confirmed.

As we pulled away from the school, my nerves began to settle. Once I had Aria and Kieran safely under John's protection, I could focus on the marble burning a hole in my pocket. Meredith had given it to me for a reason. If I could unlock its secrets, maybe I could finally meet the Callahan siblings on equal ground.

———

Quantum Creamery hit you like a child's fever dream. Holographic technology made the walls ripple with swirling stripes in every color imaginable, while the sweet scent of sugar and cream filled the air.

The moment we entered, my phone blinged. Instead of the expected message, an interactive menu materialized, asking if I wanted to order directly or receive help from a robot assistant. Before I could choose, a metallic robot in a pink-and-white striped apron approached, wielding what appeared to be a laser ice cream scoop.

"Welcome to Quantum Creamery, would you like to try our newest frozen treat?" Its mechanical voice chirped as it attempted to herd us toward a glass wall labeled "Flavor Lab."

"What is it?" Kieran jumped in before I could wave the robot off.

"Our Aurora Borealis Cone." The robot's screen-face shifted from a smile to cartoonishly wide eyes, an effect I found unsettling but clearly designed to appeal to children. "A stunning visual and taste experience, this ice cream cone features layers of aurora-inspired flavors that glow in the dark, thanks to safe, edible bioluminescent ingredients."

"Can I have that, Mom?" Kieran's voice held a note of wonder.

"Whatever you want." Aria's glance my way carried the same urgency I felt—the need to keep moving, to put distance between us and James. But the ice cream stop served its purpose, giving us both a moment to plan and keeping Kieran distracted from our real concerns.

"Can I have an Aurora Borealis Cone?" Kieran asked the robot.

I checked my watch again, calculating the minutes until John's lecture ended.

"Of course," the robot said, gesturing toward the Flavor Lab. "This way, please."

Kieran followed eagerly, mesmerized by the scene behind the glass. Robot workers in white coats moved around the lab, their screen-faces displaying exaggerated expressions of concentration as they worked. Their arms whirred softly as they mixed, poured, and experimented with an array of exotic ingredients. Above each robot's station, video displays showed magnified views of the ingredients being mixed and manipulated. The robots' screen faces occasionally changed expression, indicating satisfaction or concentration. One robot adjusted the settings on a machine that seemed to flash-freeze the ice cream using liquid nitrogen, while another wielded a laser to caramelize a sugar topping without melting the underlying scoop.

"Your order will be filled by Chef Andre." The assistant pointed to a robot sporting an absurd cartoon mustache that curled into elaborate points. "Watch now."

While Kieran stared transfixed at the treat preparation in the lab, I pulled Aria aside to a seating area furnished with chairs that resembled oversized marshmallows. Interactive tabletops flickered between games, menus, and scientific explanations of their ice cream creation process.

"I'm going to take you both to my friend, John. He can keep you safe."

"Who is John?" Confusion flickered across her face. "Why are we not coming with you?"

"He's the only person I trust here in Chicago. I've known the Tellman family my whole life."

"But we don't know him," Aria pressed.

"Trust me." A red-haired woman, a young boy, and a sheep rancher would stand out too much on Chicago's streets. Splitting up was our only option. "I have something to do, and I need to be confident you're both safe."

"What do you need to do without us?" Her voice softened. "Without me?"

The marble felt cool against my palm as I pulled it out. "I have to find out what's stored on this... the prism drive, as you called it."

"Why can't I help?" Her brows drew together, forming that familiar crease I remembered so well from Meredith.

My words caught in my throat. How could I explain my doubts about her loyalty, about the mysterious Subgroup she communicated with so easily? This tiny sphere could hold the answers I'd been seeking. "It's something I have to do alone."

"But I want to come with you." Her fingers brushed my arm.

I stared at her perfect hand—the immaculate nails, the flawless skin. So like Meredith, yet not quite. "No."

She withdrew, disappointment evident in her posture.

"Before I take you to Tellman, I need to ask you something." Better to redirect the conversation than dwell on the hurt I'd caused - hurt that an android shouldn't be capable of feeling.

"What is it?" A tinge of coldness had crept into her voice.

I'd hurt her feelings...at least that's what it felt like. But an android didn't have feelings. I shoved aside any guilt. This was about safety, about minimizing risks. "You need to disconnect from your Subgroup before I take you to my friend."

Her frown deepened, something almost like fear crossing her features. "Disconnect? But then I wouldn't know where to find you, I wouldn't be able to communicate—"

"Like at Northwestern," I reminded her, trying to gentle my tone. "You lost connection there too, remember? And everything was fine."

"It felt empty, Elijah." She gazed through the window at the oblivious passersby. "And I wouldn't be with you."

Her words, so human in their vulnerability, threatened to crack my resolve. "But what if it keeps Kieran safe?"

As if summoned, the boy bounded over, his ice cream creation casting an ethereal glow in the dimmed lights. "Look at this, Mom!"

"That's really neat," Aria managed, watching him for a moment before turning back to me, determination replacing uncertainty. "I removed my tracking device."

Her admission about disabling the tracking device startled me—not just that she'd done it without being told, but that she'd chosen to defy her programming in a way that went against everything I thought I knew about robots and their inability to act against their masters' wishes.

"I'll disconnect from the Subgroup for now, but only for Kieran's safety. If I sense he's in danger, I'll reconnect."

"Will I glow in the dark tonight after I eat this?" Kieran settled beside his robot mother.

She smiled at her son. "I guess we'll find out. Won't we?"

"Thank you, Aria." The pieces were falling into place, but success was far from certain. Next stop was the hotel to find John. After that, I'd seek out Alan's friend Katrina at the hot dog stand in Connors Park. If she truly had been Alan's confidante, perhaps she'd be willing to talk.

———

Kieran barely touched his glowing ice cream creation. He darted to the social media corner for a photo with the robot host, then waved goodbye to his new mechanical friends in the

Flavor Lab. Aria guided him toward the exit while I checked our taxi's arrival time.

"Now we will meet with John?" Aria asked as we stepped into the autumn wind that had swept across Lake Michigan and funneled between the skyscrapers.

"Yes." I flagged down an approaching yellow taxi.

Kieran bounded inside, his earlier wariness forgotten. Aria slid in after him.

As I leaned forward for the driver to scan my payment, a sleek car glided to a halt, blocking our path. The back door opened.

James Callahan.

My heart plummeted. "I thought you removed your tracker?" I whispered to Aria, glancing at Kieran, still unsure if he realized his mother's true nature.

Kieran chattered about Quantum Creamery, oblivious to the tension. I had to move fast.

"James," Aria breathed, her head dipping as her breathing quickened.

Could an android truly feel fear, or was this another programmed response to appear more human?

"Driver, back up!" Adrenaline sharpened my voice.

The robot driver shifted into reverse, but James approached with measured strides.

"Hey, that's Dad," Kieran's eyes widened. "How did he know we were here? Did you tell him, Mom? He'll be mad that I'm not in school."

Aria pulled her son close, protective.

"Go, go!"

The taxi swerved around Callahan's car and accelerated away. James's furious face diminished in the mirror. Aria's rigid posture softened as she kissed Kieran's forehead. "He's probably upset he missed out on the ice cream. We'll see him later tonight after his big presentation."

Kieran fell quiet, sensing the undercurrent of tension.

"Take us to the Drake," I instructed. The formal unveiling of Callabots loomed this afternoon—yesterday's demonstration had been only a preview. The hotel might be risky, but John remained my only option. Chicago wasn't my territory. At home, I'd have countless hiding places, friends ready to help. Here, I was adrift.

Our driver cut down a narrow alley too tight for Callahan's sedan, then merged onto a different street. The dark car was nowhere in sight.

The events replayed in my mind as we wove through traffic. James had found us too easily after the school. Had Aria truly removed her tracker? Our fragile trust wavered. Perhaps I'd let her resemblance to Meredith cloud my judgment. But Kieran wouldn't leave without his mother, and I'd sworn to protect Meredith's child. For now, I needed them both.

Aria's head came to rest on my shoulder. "Please keep us safe, Elijah. I trust you."

Her lilting alto transported me back. Meredith across our dinner table, the fading light of dusk in her eyes. "I love you," she'd said in that same voice years ago. My soul ached to believe it was real.

"I won't let anything happen to you," I promised, taking her hand. The city blurred beyond the windows as I lost myself in the soft whooshing sound of the air car, the beating of my heart, and Aria's gentle sigh against my shoulder.

CHAPTER 7
TELLMAN'S SURPRISE

ARIA, Kieran, and I waited outside the symposium session that John Tellman should be attending. A few hotel employees raised their eyebrows seeing a nine-year-old making hot chocolate at the refreshments table that was supposed to be for attending ranchers who'd paid their registration fees, but none of them said anything.

I scanned the hall in both directions expecting James Callahan to show up at any moment. His surprise appearance at the ice cream shop had me on tenterhooks.

"I am sure you are worried about James finding us here," Aria said to as we stood together a good distance from where the boy finished filling his mug. "Do you want me to connect to the Subgroup to see if they can locate him?"

"We don't need their help," I said brusquely. A team of Callabots collaborating who had all been created by Samantha and James didn't instill much confidence in our remaining undetected. "John and I can figure something out."

Before she could respond, the doors of the Lakeshore Ballroom opened and a flood of people exited. The diverse group of ranchers showcased a unique blend of traditional and business attire. Some wore smart suits that adjusted to the indoor temperature with subtly shifting colors, while others clung to classic denim and their best cowboy boots.

As they flowed into the hallway and headed for the refreshments, the group discussed the latest in gene-editing advancements for livestock that had been revealed during the session. The presence of the symposium in Chicago, far from the open fields and their animals, probably was a curious sight for the more sophisticated city dweller who probably didn't know the difference between farm raised cattle and sheep and the meat grown in a lab.

For a moment I wished I was one of them—here to enjoy meeting with people from all over the country who understood me and to learn more about how to advance my ranch and keep it going into the future. Then it dawned on me I was the last Zurbano. I had no children who would take over someday. When I was no longer able to run things, I'd probably have to shut everything down.

I spied John in the crowd and headed toward him, signaling to Aria she should remain where she was. Kieran had joined up with her blowing air across his hot drink to cool it down and seemed excited by the activity and crowd around him.

"John," I called out with a quick wave. "Do you have a minute?"

He came over. "How was your session?"

I put my hand on his shoulder and steered him toward Aria and Kieran. "I didn't attend my session this morning."

"Oh?"

My nerves kicked in. John would be the only other person in the room who would recognize Aria and believe her to be my wife come back from the dead. I didn't know how to spare him the shock. "I'd like you to meet someone."

The crowd parted, and Aria stood proud and straight, her wavy red hair rippling down her back. I tried so hard to keep these two things separate: Aria and Meredith. But as time passed, it grew more and more difficult to convince myself of the differences.

John gasped. "Meredith?" He looked at me, his brows coming together. "But how—?"

"Let's go into the ballroom, shall we?" I led my friend into the empty space that had just held several dozen symposium attendees. Kieran and Aria followed.

A couple of hotel employees were cleaning up the room—vacuuming the carpets, picking up trash, and wheeling out two carts with high-capacity automated coffee urns on them.

"Is this your friend John?" Aria asked after I shut the door.

"Who is this, Eli?" Tellman completely ignored Aria's question, but now a look of horror had overtaken his features. "What is going on?"

"I need you to stay calm." My voice was steady, but inside, turmoil churned. I knew this wasn't going to be simple, confronting the unimaginable with someone so unprepared. Yet, it was proving to be harder than I had imagined. I'd imparted a sense of rational reason on my friend without really considering how shocking the reality would be. Aria, standing there, the spitting image of my late wife, was not something you could easily rationalize.

Tellman's eyes were wide, darting between Aria and me, searching for an explanation in a situation where logic seemed to falter. His face had drained of color, as he struggled to grasp what his senses told him was impossible.

"Tellman, it's a lot to take in, I know. She's... she's not Meredith. But it's complicated," I attempted to explain, my words feeling inadequate.

"It's nice to meet you, John," Aria said, breaking the tense silence. She held out her hand, and my friend absentmindedly shook it out of pure practiced good manners. "This is my son, Kieran."

Kieran smiled and sipped on his hot chocolate.

"Why don't you sit over there," Aria said to her son pointing him in the direction of a row of chairs about ten yards away that faced the main stage. "The adults are going to chat about boring stuff."

The boy rolled his eyes and headed for the chairs.

John, still not dealing well with what was right in front of him, ignored Aria and spoke only to me. "What is this? Some kind of sick joke?" His eyes darted to the boy drinking from his mug. "Whose kid is that?"

I took a deep breath and glanced at the projection clock on the opposite wall. I didn't have a lot of time to explain things. "It's not a joke, John. Her name is Aria, and she is one of the Callabots. Remember yesterday?"

John looked Aria up and down. His brows pulled inward and his lips pressed together.

"They made her this way on purpose," I explained as my friend dealt with the shock. "She even has some of Meredith's memories."

"That can't be. How is that possible?" Then he took a step back. "Why did you bring her here? I don't understand."

There was so much to explain and not enough time. "You need to trust me, John. You've known me your whole life. Have I ever given you a reason to doubt me?"

He kept his gaze fixed on Aria.

"Someone made her, and I'm trying to find out why. There are bad people after me because of that, and I want to make sure Aria and Meredith's son are safe. But it's too dangerous if they're with me. Now do you understand?"

"That's Meredith's kid?" John peered around Aria to observe the boy who had taken a phone out of his pocket.

Dammit.

That's how his father found us at the ice cream shop. How stupid could I be?

I pushed past my friend and approached Kieran. "Hey, can I borrow your phone for a second?"

He was slumped down in his seat playing some kind of video game on it. "Why?" he asked without looking at me.

"I just need to check something."

"You have a phone, I saw it," he said in a monotone. "Why can't you use your own?"

Aria understood the problem. "Give Elijah your phone, Kieran. Now."

The boy reluctantly looked away from the screen to meet my gaze. He scowled. "This is stupid, and this place is boring. Some adventure." Then he threw his phone at me. It rolled up and softly landed on the carpet a few inches from my feet.

"Thank you." I scooped it up.

Aria took it from my hands, switched it within seconds to airplane mode, and then gave it back to her son. "No wi-fi for now. Got it?"

Kieran shot me a nasty look. "If you wanted me to put it in airplane mode, why didn't you just ask?"

Guess his joy over his ice cream treat had worn off. Now I was the jerk in the room. Great.

"Kieran," Aria said in a warning tone.

John had been very quiet during the whole exchange. Would he beg off helping me? My ask was a big one, and I hadn't explained much. As the minutes ticked away, I only had so much time to track down Katrina at the park. If I didn't find her, my whole plan would crumble.

"I'll do it," my old friend said quietly. "They can hide out in my room. I'll make sure the maid service stays away.

I let out a breath. "Thank you. I owe you one." I touched Aria on the shoulder. "Do whatever he tells you. When I return we can figure out what to do next."

She flashed a brief smile.

"I'm not doing it for you," said John. "I'm doing it for Meredith."

"Understood." The seconds ticked away. "I have to be somewhere. I'll be in touch."

John's usually sunny demeanor had shifted into something more serious. "Follow me, you two. We need to take the service elevator if we want to avoid being seen."

We went in separate directions out in the hall. Aria glanced over her shoulder as she and Kieran followed John. Tension contorted her features. I gave her an encouraging nod.

Then I strode toward the neon-lit exit sign at the far end of the building. I passed by a team of technicians and designers setting up an elaborate multi-media display for the main Callabot presentation—the reveal to the world about what Callahan, Inc. had achieved in the realm of advanced robotics.

I was running out of time.

I HEADED INTO CONNORS PARK, hoping that Alan's co-worker would be at the hot dog stand like he'd talked about at the diner. I wasn't sure if they met there every day for lunch or occasionally. But I had to try. Mature trees lined the path I'd selected and cast a pleasant shade for the warm autumn afternoon. At its center I could see a pond with a variety of food and drink stands.

A number of workers from the nearby buildings made up most of those waiting for a bite to eat in the fresh air before returning to their stagnant office spaces. I felt sorry for them locked away in giant buildings with LED lighting and recycled air circulating. My life on the ranch was a world away. As I neared the bustling food truck scene, the rich smell of fried foods and sizzling barbecue made my mouth water. Breakfast had been hours ago.

What would it hurt to buy myself a hot dog while trying to figure out if Katrina was here?

I got in line behind a couple of men who looked like construction workers with hard hats and orange high-visibility vests. So this spot wasn't only a lunch spot for the white-collar workers of Chicago.

When I reached the front of the line, I placed my order and gave the cook my name. He charged my phone, and I grabbed my frozen snythberry drink before stepping aside to let the next person in line give their order.

I scanned the people eating and waiting in line, somehow thinking I could identify a geeky female robotics expert based on looks alone. One twenty-something woman in an ill-fitting bulky sweater and wearing round-framed glasses became one possible candidate. Another was sitting alone at a table near the pond in a shapeless and unflattering dress absentmindedly scrolling through her phone while chomping on her lunch—however, it wasn't a hot dog.

Would Katrina eat more than just hot dogs here? Alan hadn't mentioned it.

"Katrina, order up!" A woman from the other end of the hot dog truck shouted out.

A pretty Asian woman in a pink pastel chiffon skirt and a white lace top embellished with pearls approached the food truck and took her order with a smile.

Not at all what I expected.

Guess she really did like the hot dogs after all.

This had to be the right person. What would be the odds?

I followed her, keeping a good ten feet of distance between us. My stomach rumbled wanting its lunch, but I tamped it down. Food could wait. This could be the only person in a city full of strangers who had the potential to help me read the data on the prism drive.

Katrina chose to sit on one of the benches. Luckily, she picked the far end. She carefully pulled her meal out of the paper bag she'd been handed, flattened it, and laid out her lunch on top of it: a hot dog piled high with cheese and onions and a bag of cricket protein crisps. Then she took out a pair of pink noise-cancelling headphones with little cat faces on them.

Before she could put them on, I took a breath to build up my courage and sat down next to her. "So are those any good?" I pointed at the bag of chips. We didn't see much of that kind of thing in Idaho. We liked traditional snacks like potato chips or popcorn.

She raised a brow. "Um."

Guess she wasn't used to being approached by older men in the park at lunch. Time to go for it. "You're Katrina, right? You work at Callahan, Inc.?"

A look of shock spread across her smooth-skinned face. "Excuse me? Who are you?" She scooted to the very edge of the bench to put more distance between us.

"I'm friends with Alan Honeycutt." I tried to give a friendly smile. "He mentioned you both worked together in robotics a while back."

"Alan." Her face paled. She started packing up her lunch, shoving the uneaten hot dog into the bag, its condiments spilling everywhere. "I don't know who you are—" She glanced around as if she were scared we'd be seen together.

She was freaking out. Not good. I needed to get her to trust me. But how? "My name is Eli Zurbano. The Callahans created an android replica of my wife, and I'm here to stop them for doing it to someone else."

Katrina paused, her movements halting mid-action as she processed my words. The mention of the Callahans and an android replica seemed to strike a chord, her eyes flickering with recognition. "The Callahans?" she echoed, her voice dropping to a whisper. "I was hoping this day would never come." She glanced up at me. "How did you find me? And why should I believe any of this?"

I sensed the shift in her, the slight crack in her armor. "Alan gave me your name and told me you two used to meet here for lunch. He said you were one of the best in the robotics department before... before you took a different job." I showed her my marble, a piece of technology that was so cutting-edge only someone in her field would recognize it. "I need to figure out what's on this drive, and I think you're the one person who can help me."

Katrina stared at it, a torrent of emotions crossing her face. Seeing the prism drive for the first time, a technology that had only been conceptual before today, a glimmer of fascination appeared.

Finally, she let out a slow breath, setting her lunch aside. "Sit down," she said, her voice steadier now, the initial shock giving way to the inquisitive scientist and engineer she once was. "If what you're saying is true, then we have a lot to discuss. But I need to know everything. Starting with how you got involved with the Callahans and why they targeted your wife."

I hadn't been expecting to tell anyone the details of my life, much less someone I'd only met a few moments ago in a park in Chicago. I closed my fist around the marble, the last connection I had to Meredith. "I never intended to get mixed up with the Callahans. I didn't know who they were—James and Samantha. I'm a rancher from a thousand miles away in town for a conference. I think they lured me here, but probably never thought I'd see her. I mean, what were the odds I'd find out that my wife, Meredith, was really Aria Callahan?"

Her eyes widened.

I gave Katrina the quick details of what had happened since I saw Aria on the street, down to the last moment I saw Alan climbing into a red air taxi just hours before his 'accident.' She took dainty bites of her hot dog, somehow managing not to drop any chili on her fluffy pink skirt. I purposefully excluded how Aria and I escaped Kieran's school and that they were both in hiding. Katrina was still a stranger to me, after all.

"When I figured out my wife had given me a prism drive before she died and used to be on the leading edge of robotics technology, I thought maybe this was what James and his sister had been after. Something on this little thing—" I opened my hand, and the marble glowed green once again. "—made them come after me, try to drain my brain like all those other people." I swallowed, thinking of the long line of desperate Chicagoans who had no idea they'd had their brains damaged by the 'medical study' they'd participated in for a measly five hundred dollars.

Her eyes grew round at the glow. "I thought prism drives were merely theoretical—only the biggest labs in the country have the tech to even attempt this." She held out her hand. "Can I take a closer look at it?"

I hesitated. Now that I suspected this was the thing the Callahans wanted so badly, to hand it over to someone else made my stomach churn. "Can you help me access the data on it?" I avoided her question, not ready to relinquish possession—especially in such a public space.

She frowned and picked up her drink instead and took a sip. "The only way I can think of to even try to extract data would require the use of a quantum computer."

"Do they have a quantum computer at Callahan, Inc.?"

Her face paled. "I don't know who you believed was involved in Alan's death, but after listening to the news and finding out the crazy stuff they're trying to link him to, I don't feel comfortable hacking into a system at work. I'm still worried someone might figure out Alan and I maintained a friendship after they kicked us out of the robotics lab. I liked him. He was a smart guy. We both missed the work we'd been doing before Samantha shut down the department and used to discuss different theories. It made us both feel as if we were still involved in something important."

"Why did James Callahan wanted a robot copy of my wife? Is that the kind of important work you thought you'd be involved in?"

"No." She set down the last few bites of her hot dog as if she'd become suddenly nauseous.

"When did you realize the Callahans were scanning brains to make their robots appear almost human?"

"I—I didn't know."

"Alan said you told him about the new medical device your company was developing," I said.

"I didn't realize what it was for, that's why I told Alan about it. I thought he might have a clue. It didn't make any sense when I heard about it through the grapevine at work."

I leaned forward, my interest piqued. "At some point he figured it out. He didn't mention the Callahans had involved him in the testing on West 22nd Street?

Katrina shook her head, her expression turning somber. "No. Until the news report this morning about the raid and the car accident, I thought Alan was running the visitors' program and doing stupid errands for Samantha on an engineer's salary." Her voice trailed off.

The look on her face made me believe she was telling the truth. Although Alan had been up to his ears in the less-than-legal actions going on behind the scenes at Callahan, Inc., it seemed that Katrina was uninvolved. Could that be the reason she was still sitting out here in a public park enjoying her lunch, rather than lying on a slab in the morgue next to her co-worker?

"Do you think it's possible to scan a brain and put it on a prism drive?" Theories had been rattling around in my mind since that conversation with Alan and the discovery that my marble was more than just a marble.

"Where are you going with this?" A wrinkle appeared in her brow.

"I think this marble holds my wife's missing memories. Memories that James and Samantha might kill to retrieve."

She stuffed the rest of her lunch into the paper bag. "I'm sorry. I can't help you."

CHAPTER 9
SOPHISTICATED PUZZLE

I STOOD, unwilling to let her leave without agreeing to help. I had nowhere else to turn and time was running out. What information did my wife want to keep from James Callahan? It must be important if she wanted to hide it from him and if he was willing to steal it from me. "Alan risked his life to save me." I touched her gently on the arm to stop her from leaving. "Are you going to make his sacrifice worthless?" It was true, if Alan hadn't stepped in and gotten me out of the brain scan, would I even be here talking to her?

Katrina's face fell, and she studied the people on the path crossing in front of us, perhaps hoping to find a friendly face and a way out of answering my question. "Please leave me alone."

She shook off my hand and strode toward a garbage can into which she stuffed her half-finished lunch. The receptacle flashed red, and a voice announced, "Food items cannot be placed in the recyclable bin. Food items cannot be placed in the recyclable bin."

She backed away from it, but it was too late, a robot park monitor wearing a blue-and-white uniform, zoomed toward her from the circle of food trucks in the center of the park. "Incorrect disposal detected. Please identify yourself."

Katrina's eyes met mine, a flash of fear—or was it defiance? —in them.

Before the robot could catch up to her, I grabbed her hand, and we ran down the path together in the opposite direction of the food trucks and curious on-lookers who were finishing up their lunches. We dodged between benches and leaped over low hedges, the robot's persistent beeps echoing behind us.

I glanced at Katrina. The trust between us was thin, yet in the chase, we were bound by a common goal: escape.

The path forked ahead, leading to the dense heart of the park on one side and the bustling city streets on the other. Without slowing, Katrina veered toward the trees. I followed, trusting her knowledge. Behind us, the robot's progress was hindered by natural obstacles. These older models didn't do so well navigating terrain that wasn't paved paths or concrete sidewalks.

When our lungs burned as much as our legs, the sound of the pursuing robot began to fade. He must've given up on trying to lay a fine on Katrina for her garbage offense. We collapsed under the cover of a large oak, its colorful autumn leaves shielding us from any prying eyes. Panting, we shared a wary glance, and the adrenaline slowly ebbed from my veins. Briefly, we were allies, united against a common foe.

Katrina smiled at me and laughed. "I hate those stupid things. A hundred dollar fine for throwing away trash? They don't recycle most of that stuff anyway—no market for it. They're just trying to keep us from using the park." She stood and brushed the sticks and leaves from her puffy skirt. "Guess us worker bees offend the muckety mucks who like to come here to enjoy the same stuff we like: trees, flowers, the pond."

She gestured at the high buildings all around us that were filled with penthouses and executive suites. "As if nature is only allowed to be enjoyed by the rich."

Somehow the act of inciting the robot into action changed things between us. "Will you help me?" I asked. "I think my wife was trying to tell me something, and I need to find out what it is."

Turning back to me, her expression hardened. "That world up there," she continued, "is built on foundations we can't even imagine, let alone access. The rich in this city live in the clouds, playing by a set of rules we'll never see. Alan got in the way, and they thought they could just squash him like a bug. As if he was nobody..."

"Then let's do something about it. If the Callahans are playing by their own set of rules, let's shake them up. Let's find out what my wife hid on the prism drive and try to level the playing field."

Katrina's jaw tightened. "You're right," she said, her voice firmer now. "The Callahans, and everyone like them, they live in their towers, manipulating lives as if they're gods among ants. It's time someone reminded them they're not above everything."

She stood, her gaze no longer on the penthouses but locked with mine. "If what's on that prism drive can truly make a difference, then yes, I'm with you. Let's expose them for what they are."

As we stood on a far street corner some distance from the food stands and the automated authorities in Connors Park, Katrina used her taxi app to hail us a ride. "I think I know someone who could help us: Dr. Liu. He's the dean of the Robotics Department these days, but when I was a student at Northwestern, he taught a class about emerging technologies. Alan and I met in that class, even though he didn't remember me at the time."

I gave her a surprised stare.

"I was super nerdy back then, sat in the back row, hardly talked to a soul. After I graduated, I figured out how to tap into the non-nerd side." She clasped her cat-head decorated pink headphones in her hands and noticed my gaze dart to them. "For the most part, anyway."

A sleek black air taxi pulled up to the curb. A luxury vehicle with gold accents and polished to a mirror shine.

"I know what you're thinking: fancy, right?" Katrina tapped on her phone screen to accept the ride. "It's a little extra, but we didn't have to wait as long. Post-lunch traffic is the worst."

I opened the door for her, and she slid into the leather back seat. "Thanks."

I joined her.

She already was giving the robot driver specific instructions about where on the Northwestern campus we wanted to go. The building name sounded familiar—I'd probably read about it in the Visitor's Center. The door automatically shut with a quiet whoosh before I could pull it closed then locked with a solid clunk. A clear container filled with cold drinks slid out from between our seats. Guess even a less prestigious position at Callahan, Inc. still paid well if Katrina felt comfortable splurging on such a ride.

As Katrina grabbed the bright-blue can of an ElectroBerry Surge from the container, white smoke from the dry ice used to cool the drinks poured out. "Please, have something. It's part of the fee. Might as well take advantage."

I scanned the choices and decided on a bottle of spring water with essence of lime and tangerine. The closest to a drink I could recognize. Kemper Creek didn't have weird drinks and fancy robot cars. Hard to believe how different rural life was compared to Chicago. A huge chasm existed between what was considered the norm here in the city compared to home.

"So tell me more about Dr. Liu and why you think he could help." I took a sip of my drink, and it was more refreshing than I'd imagined it would be.

"Well, for one, I was an A student in his class and graduated summa cum laude. He specifically requested to hand me my diploma on graduation day." She gave a brief and uncomfortable smile, which made me think she wasn't used to bragging about herself in this way. "He has access to the quantum computer lab at the university and probably knows more than anyone about prism drive theory."

"Theory?" I pulled my marble out of my pocket. "I think it's not a theory anymore."

"Can I?" Her eyes widened as the object glowed green and lit up the inside of the cab.

Last time she'd asked, we'd been sitting on a park bench, and I worried about giving it up to her. But here in the taxi she had nowhere to go. "Sure."

When the marble touched her palm, the green light immediately was extinguished. The interior of the marble that had always looked like a night sky with stars in it, turned gray and misty.

"Oh," she exclaimed and turned it over in her hand. "Why did it change?"

"I don't know." I was perplexed the marble turned such a strange shade of gray. For years it had been in my marble collection with the same appearance—its color had never changed. Now in the last twenty-four hours, not only had the marble glowed, it had shifted color completely. "It's never done that before."

"Interesting." Katrina rolled it across her palm with a single finger, examining it quietly, then handed it back to me. "It makes me want to get back to doing work that matters again. At first, I thought any job with Callahan, Inc. was better than downgrading to a company with a lesser reputation. After a few years I was hoping they'd forget why they kicked me out of the robotics program, and I'd be invited back." She sighed. "Drone engineering is not how I envisioned my career."

When the marble landed back in my palm, the glow returned stronger than ever.

She shook her head at the rapid change. "Wow, what I wouldn't give to be part of a team working on prism technology. Truly fascinating stuff."

It pleased me that the marble seemed to react only to my touch and no one else's. Could it be that I was the only person in the world Meredith truly trusted, besides her own child? After my experiences in Chicago, I could see why. People she'd loved and depended on had turned on her—even her husband and Samantha, her college best friend.

"Could my wife have made this by herself?" Maybe this had been a secret project all her own. The Visitor's Center display and everything I was able to glean online about Meredith and her background pointed to a genius-level mind.

Katrina frowned. "She'd need a very sophisticated lab to create it. It's not as if you can just whip up a prism drive in your garage or something."

I snorted a laugh and remembered a time when I'd been wrestling with the obstinate engine of my granddad's old tractor in the barn. As I'd wiped the sweat from my brow,

Meredith had approached, quietly observing my struggle with a curious tilt of her head.

"You know," she'd begun in a casual tone, "if you recalibrate the fuel injection timing, it might do the trick. The manual suggested it as something often overlooked."

I had paused, tools in hand, and looked up at her, genuinely taken aback. She had offered a solution that was both technically precise and brilliantly simple.

For a short time, I remember simply staring—my wife was an enigma. It wasn't only the suggestion she'd made, but the way her eyes had sparkled and how a faint smile had played on her lips, as if she'd shared a secret part of herself for the first time.

"Why didn't you tell me you knew about this stuff?" I'd asked.

Meredith shrugged. "I've always loved puzzles. And you, my dear, are the most interesting puzzle of all."

Katrina didn't know my wife at all. But that was all right. She'd take me to someone who could help unlock whatever puzzle Meredith had left behind for me. How ironic that the husband who couldn't always figure out how to fix things and make them run again would be left with a technological mystery: a marble infused with secrets that could change everything. It was almost laughable, really, that Meredith with her brilliant mind had entrusted me, a man who occasionally fumbled with the workings of a tractor, to unravel the riddle she had buried inside this tiny sphere.

She had always seen more in me than I had seen in myself, though, and had always believed I possessed a certain kind of wisdom that the modern world often overlooked. The marble wasn't a test of my intellect, but it was a testament to our love. She knew me so well that she had been confident I would figure out the truth that had eluded others. Even James had no idea my marble was more than a marble—and they'd had the opportunity to snatch it out of my hands more than once.

"Meredith could do anything she put her mind to," I said.

The taxi hummed quietly as it navigated through the bustling streets, the silence between us stretching as Katrina digested my words. She was just the latest tool in my search for answers. I'd use anyone, risk anything, to uncover what Meredith had buried in this marble—and why she'd trusted me, of all people, to keep it safe.

CHAPTER 10
TURING'S ACOLYTES

AS THE LUXURY taxi drove us through the heart of Northwestern, it used a different street than the one I remembered from my first visit. Buildings rushed past that looked unfamiliar to me—a blend of old and new. As it was a little past the lunch hour, campus was filled with students walking in all directions, some leaving what appeared to be a central cafeteria named Sargent Dining Hall and others heading into buildings labeled as the Technological Institute and the College of Community and Cultural Studies. Others entered the Sargent Residence Hall, rode e-bikes, or walked under trees raining down red and orange leaves in the brisk lake breeze.

"I get that it sounds weird," said Katrina, taking the last sip of her ElectroBerry Surge and depositing the recyclable bottle into a trash container that magically popped out of the center console between the robot driver and the passenger seat, "but I haven't been on campus in years. Everything looks so, well, smaller than I remember it. The students look a lot younger, too."

A horde of young women wearing HoloBracelets went past. I'd seen ads for them on the billboards all over the city and even on the streamed news channel in the hotel lobby. Guess they were the latest rage. I'd have to bring a couple back for some ranch neighbors to give to their teenage daughters. They'd probably be over the moon. The HoloBracelets were sleek, adjustable bands that projected life-sized holographic images, as I understood it. The female students on the street were projecting holographs of what appeared to be their family dogs—one was a white poodle, another an Irish Wolfhound, and still a third was some kind of mixed-up terrier with beady eyes. Even though the dogs were only projected images, students either walking or riding by on the other side of the street, swerved out of the way to avoid hitting the holographic animals.

"And dumber," Katrina finished.

The taxi slowed to a stop after a turn onto Tech Drive. "We have arrived at your destination," the robot driver said in its wooden voice.

Katrina leaned forward so the driver could charge her phone. "Thank you."

It seemed strange to thank a robot that didn't even have legs, but humans still wanted to have polite, normal interactions even with machines.

The doors popped open, and we both stepped out. A smattering of light rain began to fall. The nice Indian summer day was giving way to more autumn-like weather.

Katrina didn't seem to be worried about her fluffy skirt or delicate blouse. Instead, she headed toward the main entrance of the Technological Institute. It was as if the nerd inside came out and grew unconcerned with appearance—her artfully styled hair melted, delicate make-up smudged, and even her mycelium shoes, a fungus-based recyclable material, began to fall apart.

"Come on," she urged me up the steps. "If I know Dr. Liu, I know exactly where he'll be after lunch before his two o'clock class."

I ran up the stairs after her. She climbed them faster than I expected her to, taking the steps two at a time. Somehow the idea of helping me figure out what was stored on the prism drive in my pocket had lit a fire under her. Better to take advantage of it before she changed her mind.

We entered the massive white building and were instantly faced with hallways and stairs and doors. Katrina didn't even pause and maneuvered with amazing dexterity through a crowd of students.

"This way," she said, leading me to a set of stairs and then down a brightly lit hall to an unlabeled door that only had an electronic notepad with a math problem on it. After knocking on it, she picked up the dangling stylus and solved it just as the door opened.

A tall Asian man in his fifties, who had hair peppered with gray and wore rimless glasses, appeared. The lab coat he wore over a crisply ironed shirt and khaki slacks bore navy blue stitching that read: Dr. Simon Liu. The minute he recognized Katrina he smiled.

"Ms. Cho, how wonderful to see you." He swung the door wide to make room for us both to enter the large office beyond. "Come in, please, and bring your friend." He nodded at me and made me feel instantly accepted into his academic world.

He noticed the writing on the notepad. "I've had that problem up there for a month now, not a single student of mine could solve it." The middle-aged professor shut the door and then said to me, "Since Ms. Cho graduated, I have yet to meet a student with the same level of intelligence." Then he ushered us into two padded chairs that faced his organized desk stacked high with an interesting collection of items: 3D printed objects in various stages of completion, circuit boards, a robotic hand model, a vintage robot toy collection, and an intriguing desktop holographic display showing what looked to be a robotic neural network in great detail.

"Dr. Liu, we are hoping you can provide us with some help." Katrina kicked off her squishy mycelium shoes in order to dry her wet feet on the throw rug. "This is my friend, Eli, and he has something that might interest you."

"Oh?" Dr. Liu pushed his glasses up his nose, tented his fingers, and focused his gaze on me. "Is this a work-related project? I can't help with anything that might violate your employment agreement."

Katrina nodded at me, and I retrieved my marble from my pocket.

"Can you help us identify what's contained on this prism drive?" I asked.

Dr. Liu's leaned back in his chair, astonishment clear on his face. "Where did you get that?"

As my marble glowed in my hand, I shifted my gaze toward Katrina. Could I really trust this stranger? A glance at the clock sharpened my resolve; the worldwide robot reveal was mere hours away, and time was a luxury I couldn't afford. The recent raid on the brain scan setup only deepened the mystery. How long before the investigators uncovered the truth? That it wasn't Alan Honeycutt at the helm of this sinister project?

Callahans' new technology darkened my thoughts. Their revolutionary robots, with capabilities beyond ordinary comprehension, threatened to eclipse everything else. Would the world even care about the origins of this technology once dazzled by its potential?

Holding the prism drive in my fist, I felt the sting of ignorance. My wife's expertise in robotics, those clandestine brain scans, the enigmatic marble—all these elements were pieces of a puzzle I couldn't solve without her insights. The Callahans, armed with knowledge of my wife's past, were moving against me with chilling precision. Even Katrina seemed to hold keys to parts of Meredith that remained shrouded from me.

"Let him look at it, Eli," she urged. "We need his help."

I stretched out my hand and dropped my marble into the delicate hand of Dr. Liu. "A gift from my wife a couple of years ago." The glow faded once it left my palm. "I thought it was a marble to add to my collection."

The professor held the now gray object between two fingers and held it up to the fluorescent lights above. "Who was your wife? This tech is only speculative." Then as if he'd spied something within the tiny sphere that captured his attention, he leapt up and headed to a flat-panel display screen on the opposite end of his office. Below the screen was a control panel with numerous knobs and buttons.

I followed him to the mystery screen. "Aria Delaney."

As he turned on the machine, Dr. Liu started at the name. "Your wife was a preeminent expert in robotics when she was here at the university, but I thought she'd eschewed this kind of advanced stuff. Something about how we shouldn't play God." He placed the marble underneath the screen and attached a sticky probe to it.

"What are you doing?" The marble was the only connection I had to my wife. What if he destroyed it with his tinkering?

"This is a digital oscilloscope," explained Katrina in a soothing tone. "He's just determining if there are any electrical signals inside the object."

"Well, it glows when I touch it now, so..." I gave her a hard stare. Would a marble glow if it didn't have some kind of electronics inside? Even a rural rube like me understood the basics of electricity.

The marble returned to its original state—a miniature night sky with colored stars sparkling.

Dr. Liu studied the information that appeared on the screen, which was a series of waveforms. To me, it meant nothing. "It's alive," he said awestruck. "No one has ever proven that prism drive technology could even be achieved. It's all still theoretical—at least in the academic world."

Then I caught on to something he'd said only minutes before. "In what way do you mean Aria 'eschewed' advanced tech?" All I'd learned about her since I arrived that she was far more advanced than many in her understanding of robotics and other speculative technologies. The Visitor's Center sung her praises, and everyone I met seemed to think she had genius-level intelligence.

"Look at this waveform, Katrina." Dr. Liu ignored my question and stared at the screen. "That's a multi-layered fractal pattern. Aria's work progressed well beyond what I thought capable last time I worked with her. I wonder why she never presented it at the Innovatech Summit last year."

"She died eighteen months ago." I focused on the screen wishing I could understand what Dr. Liu and Katrina marveled at. She was my wife, and I didn't have any idea what she was capable of—the brilliant mind behind the gentle, sweet woman I remembered.

"Impossible. I heard she was at the Visitor's Center the other day," said the professor.

"That was a robot replica of Aria Delaney." I reached for the cord and unplugged the oscilloscope and the screen went black. Both Dr. Liu and Katrina reeled back. "James Callahan and his sister have been pawning her off as the real thing for a while now."

"You're joking." Dr. Liu smirked and blew air out his nose. "Where did you find this guy?" He looked to my companion. "Are you sure it's really his prism drive?"

"He's not lying professor." Her gaze lifted slowly, a knowing look in her eyes. "I always wondered why Aria never seemed quite the same after she returned from her sabbatical. Now it all makes sense."

"I don't have time to deal with this," I spat out. The news about Aria being a robot was probably shocking to them both, but they'd have to save their questions and speculations for another time. "Later today the Callahans are going to reveal more of these robots to the world, and the tech will be out there. Once people see how advanced the Callabots are, nobody is going to care where they came from. Think about when Oppenheimer and Fermi created the atom bomb and how that went." I ripped off the sticky probe attached to my marble, and it glowed green again in my hand, as if my wife was calling to me from beyond the grave. "I need your help to figure out what information my wife hid on this thing. James Callahan broke into my hotel room to find it then tried to send me into some secret brain scan machine, so who knows what he might do next."

Dr. Liu processed my words, retreating into his scientific mindset with a clinician's detachment. "Although my understanding of prism drive technology is based on speculative papers and theories only, I think I can attempt to decode what's on it." He looked to Katrina. "I'll need your help."

"Of course, professor." The former Callahan robotics employee's eyes glowed at the request. "I never thought I'd have an opportunity like this again."

The professor headed to his desk, opened a drawer, and pulled out an old-fashioned metal key. "The quantum computer lab should be empty right now. Students have to sign up with a mentor and there are only limited sessions. The power consumption is ridiculous and with the university's requirement to reduce student energy use by forty percent this year, it's getting harder and harder for projects to be approved. Luckily, faculty don't have to follow such strict rules." His keen, inquisitive eyes snapped with excitement. "I have an appointment in an hour or so. Maybe we can crack it before then."

When we left Liu's office and headed to the lab, I brought up the topic once again about his reference to my wife not having an interest in advanced tech. "You never answered my question about Aria. Why did you think she shunned advanced tech? I thought she was one of the most honored alumnae here at Northwestern because of her research and her accomplishments in advanced concepts."

"I told Aria I wouldn't involve myself in her affiliations when I found out," he said. "It wasn't really my place to tell her how to view technology. I respected her as a fellow scientist who displayed an intelligence that far surpassed mine. But at some point, her views changed dramatically. One day I was a trusted colleague who she would call on occasion to bounce off her latest theories and the next she was talking about Turing's Acolytes and how they would be the ones to save us from ourselves."

"Turing's Acolytes?" I asked. I knew that Turing was considered one of the fathers of artificial intelligence due to his development of the Turing Test, a method for determining whether a machine can exhibit intelligent behavior indistinguishable from that of a human. But that was the extent of my knowledge.

"You've heard the term 'Luddite' before?" Katrina said, scanning the hall for anyone who might overhear.

"You mean the people who started that fire at the library?" The last time I remember hearing that term, Persephone, our tour guide, had been explaining how some of the damage to the archives probably was because of some group of Luddites. I hadn't thought anything more about it and wrote it off as the typical 'radicals' who like to destroy things rather than create them. But Meredith? An arsonist? It didn't make sense.

She nodded. "That was Turing's Acolytes. They'd spray painted it on the wall inside the library lobby. They're a shadowy group of former scientists and researchers who think we are headed down the wrong path when it comes to technology and artificial intelligence."

"I've never heard of them." The irony of the name struck me; Turing's own legacy was now entangled with a group that might well be seeking to dismantle the very advancements he had pioneered. But why would Meredith be part of such a group? Maybe this better explained why she'd ended up at the end of my driveway one snowy day years ago.

"I'm not surprised. The authorities like to pretend they don't exist or at least that they haven't done much damage," explained Katrina. "They think this will keep the general public calm and focused on more positive things. Who wants to believe a group of super-smart people who are supposed to be the ones advancing society are the ones who actually want to destroy it? That's a scary concept for most."

Dr. Liu stopped in front of a door with a fingerprint scanning device next to the handle "When Aria found out I didn't support her views on technology, she cut off all ties. That's why I was so surprised when you showed up in my office claiming she'd created a prism drive." His mouth tightened, and he glanced at me. "I didn't want to report her possible connection to the fire because of the public scandal—Aria has been revered by the university and many other academic institutions for her discoveries. Revealing her involvement with such fringe people might damage the research we've been doing as a result of her work. Someone might shut us down just because her name is attached to some of our discoveries. I couldn't risk it." He pressed his index finger to the scanner, the door beeped, and he opened it to reveal a second door into which he fit the metal key. "Besides, they put out the fire quickly. It didn't cause much damage. Since then, we haven't had any more activity on campus like that. They've moved onto to bigger targets I think."

Once past the locked door, the quantum computer room was dominated by a massive machine housed within a glass case. A puff of very cold air, carrying a clean, metallic scent assaulted my nose. Soft blue and purple lights shone inside the case casting a strange glow. A constant, low hum emanated from the box, which was punctuated by the occasional higher-pitched whine of cooling fans.

"Say hello to Maxwell, our quantum computer," said Katrina.

"Hello, Katrina. Hello Dr. Liu," said a strange, smooth voice with a deliberate cadence. "How may I assist you today?"

The computer was talking to us.

CHAPTER 11
ARIA

JOHN TELLMAN CHECKED the locks on the door, then the windows, then back to the door again. His movements were quick, restless. On the way up in the service elevator, he'd projected a strange calm, but now that illusion had cracked.

Aria scanned his expression several times as he strode past her and Kieran while they sat calmly on the bed.

Furrowed brow. Tightness around mouth. Gaze darting around the room.

She didn't need to scan her databanks very long to decipher the man was worried.

"Are we safe here?" She was bothered by Elijah's insistence that she disconnect from Gwen and the Subgroup. With access, she could easily scan their incoming data to pinpoint James and Samantha's whereabouts. The Callabot presentation was only an hour away. Despite her husband's eagerness to find her and her son, James wouldn't risk missing his moment in the spotlight when the curtain rose on the show.

John paused in his third check of the door lock. "I don't think anyone saw us get in that service elevator and the hall was empty. But there are cameras everywhere. Would the Callahans have access to those?"

"Perhaps." John did not understand the brilliance of James and Samantha, nor their creations. The Callabots could do practically anything the siblings commanded them to do. Only Aria seemed capable of independent reasoning. A flaw, perhaps, in her programming? Or the way she was made? She was, after all, the first creation. She understood that now.

"Shit." The younger rancher ran a hand through his short blond hair. "What the hell are we supposed to do?"

That was not appropriate language for a child.

As Aria stood, her movements were precise and measured, reflecting the calculated grace of her engineering. She fixed her gaze squarely on John. Crossing the room, she stopped a respectful distance from him. "I request that you do not use cursing around my son. That is completely unacceptable."

John backed away with widened eyes. "Hey, back off."

Did he not understand that she wouldn't hurt a friend of Elijah's? She only wanted to correct his inappropriate language. Wouldn't any mother do the same?

"She's not going to hurt you," said Kieran from his spot on the bed. "Her programming won't let her." He set aside his phone and the game he was playing to look at them both. "She's my mother. Don't you get it?"

Her mind grabbed onto Kieran's words. It shocked her that he knew. He understood her nature. Ever since she'd awakened and found Kieran clinging to her, she had embraced the role of mother, guided solely by her programmed instincts. A profound loyalty and love had blossomed the moment he took her hand. Until now, she had never questioned his emotions or actions; he was her son, and she was his mother. That simplicity had been enough—until Kieran's words hinted at a deeper understanding.

But a boy at seven is much different from a boy at nine.

A boy at nine becomes wiser. He learns that Santa Claus isn't real. That people die and don't come back. That trust should be earned and not given outright.

Kieran recognized she was not human, but still accepted her as his mother. A warmth radiated through her circuits at the revelation.

"If you are worried about the cameras," she said. "I could access the system from here and corrupt any video that exists." Elijah wouldn't approve of the idea. He'd worry it was too risky, exposing them to discovery by activating anything that might send out a detectable signal.

"You can?" The lines in John's forehead smoothed at the suggestion.

"Yes." And then she would also connect one more time to the Subgroup to see where the danger lay. Only then could she be satisfied her son was safe, that no one would find them unless she wanted to be found.

"What's that?" Kieran's voice snapped their attention back to him. He was sitting on the bed, his eyes fixed on the old-fashioned phone on the nightstand, intrigued by the red light that flashed intermittently.

John hurried over to it. "That means I have a voicemail message. It could be someone from back home wondering why I haven't called or texted in a while. My phone was stolen," he explained. He pressed on the voice mail button and the tinny speaker came to life.

"You're making a grave mistake, John," James Callahan's voice came through, cold and menacing. "Harboring them isn't just foolish—it's dangerous. Consider this your final warning. Back out now or face the consequences."

CHAPTER 12
TRUSTING MEREDITH

"GOOD AFTERNOON, MAXWELL," said Dr. Liu to the inanimate object under the glass box. His voice came off cheerful, as if he were addressing a good friend he hadn't seen in a while. "We have a very interesting task for you today."

The gray walls must have been lined with noise-dampening panels, as Dr. Liu's words vanished into the silence. Around the edges, banks of auxiliary computers and monitors hummed, their screens alive with data streams. Meredith in her former life had thrived in such a technical environment. Now, stepping into this unfamiliar territory felt akin to navigating an unknown forest while hunting elk—utterly out of my element, yet I was here, reliant on this technology to unravel the mysteries surrounding my wife.

"I love interesting tasks, doctor," said the quantum computer. "How can I help you?"

"I have with me a prism drive—"

"Prism drives only exist in theory," the computer cut him off abruptly. "I'm sorry, Dr. Liu, I cannot help you."

Dr. Liu held the marble between his thumb and forefinger and presented it to what looked like a small camera on the exterior of the clear box. "Please scan the item to determine that this is a functioning prism drive."

The computer beeped and whirred. A red light on the side of the small camera glowed.

I stood back and watched as my favorite marble, which had been dropped in the mud one spring, lost in the snow after a rough ATV ride to check on a newborn lamb, and even used a few times in my slingshot to take pot shots at the annoying magpie who wouldn't leave the robin's nest alone in my front pasture, was scanned. I didn't realize the importance and specialness of that chunk of glass. If I had, I would've treated it with a lot more care.

"I apologize Dr. Liu," said the computer after a few seconds of scanning. "You are correct, this is a prism drive. In theory, it allows micro-crystals to exist in multiple states simultaneously, so that vast amounts of information can be stored."

"Yes, Maxwell, I know what a prism drive is." Dr Liu smiled wryly. "I was hoping you could read the data on it."

"I can attempt to read the data," said the computer in its flat voice. "But providing an output may be impossible without the correct protocol for which the data was built. Place the drive on my interface, please."

On one side of the box a sleek, glassy tray popped out. Under its transparent surface an intricate network of fine, metallic circuits was visible, which glowed with an iridescent shimmer. Dr. Liu placed my marble on the tray, and it instantly shone even more brightly than when it was in my hand. The tray pulsed, and a low buzz filled the small room.

"What's happening?" I asked Katrina in a reverential whisper. I felt as though I were witnessing something magical taking place.

"Maxwell is trying to read the device," she explained.

Excitement radiated from her. "A prism drive is like a mini-quantum computer. They should be able to communicate, but since we don't know how the drive was created or how it was encoded, it might be impossible. All we can do is hope."

Were all of my wife's memories stored on the device? Or only her theoretical work and formulas destroyed by Turing's Acolytes? Would she really leave the marble in my possession if I couldn't understand what was on it?

She'd given it to me with a smile, as if she were indulging my childhood passion for collecting marbles. Was that really the attitude of someone who wanted the data to be found and read and used?

"I'm not so sure about this," I said, a growing unease tightening in my chest. Everything I'd learned in the last few days had tarnished my memories of her. Was this truly honoring her last wishes? Should I just leave everything as it was? Meredith could have never imagined that I'd encounter her robot twin. "I want you to stop," I said.

"Dr. Liu, should I continue to read the prism drive?" asked the quantum computer that appeared almost sentient with its glowing exterior and strange human-like voice. Each word it spoke rippled across with lights brightening and dimming to match the emphasis in a phrase.

Katrina looked at me, and a frown pulled at the corners of her mouth. "You asked for my help. We wouldn't be here if you didn't beg me to do it."

"I don't remember begging." My face flushed hot. I was torn, wanting to discover the drive's secrets, while at the same time fearing them. Would I be unleashing something my wife had wanted hidden forever?

She must've read my face—the uncertainty flowing through me. "Dr. Liu, can we take a minute?" Katrina asked.

"Of course." The middle-aged professor dipped his head in acknowledgment, then addressed the computer, "Maxwell, please pause in your analysis."

"System paused," said the computer.

Katrina pulled me to the far side of the room where the hums of processors and the whir of the air conditioner cooling the small space formed a private bubble.

"What's going on?" she asked. "You look scared. I told you Dr. Liu is trustworthy. He won't betray us to anyone."

"I'm not worried about betrayal," I said. "What if there's something on the drive that isn't supposed to be out in the world? When I met my wife, I knew nothing about her life out here. I didn't even know her real name, her connection to the Callahan family, or her work in robotics. She kept me in the dark for a reason."

"But she gave this 'marble' to you," Katrina reasoned. "Nobody else but you. Doesn't that mean she trusted you with whatever might be hidden on it?"

"I'm not sure. Maybe she thought I'd never figure it out or maybe it was all about maintaining control over something." I sighed, recalling the doctor's revelation. "Dr. Liu told us a little while ago she'd joined up with a group that hated technology so much they damaged the university archives and tried to burn down the library, for God's sake. Who was my wife? Was she even the person I thought I married? Was all of it a lie?"

"Eli, please, try to calm down," she urged softly, her hand reaching out to steady my arm. "I don't think it's like that at all. Think about the marble's reaction when you handed it to me. It changed color. It only glowed when you held it."

"So?" I was skeptical yet intrigued.

Her expression brightened. "That has to be significant. I was thinking about it on the way here in the taxi. How could that be possible? Could an object identify who held it? Be programmed to turn on when the right person was meant to access it?"

Dr. Liu who had been quietly adjusting some equipment, suddenly chimed in. So much for our private conversation. "I suspect it's a combination of Delayed Activation Protocol and Quantum Entanglement. Quite ingenious, really."

"Fascinating." Katrina's dark eyes lit up.

Feeling lost, I asked, "Can someone please explain what you two are talking about please? A quantum what?"

Before Dr. Liu could answer, the quantum computer must have assumed I was addressing it and began to speak, "A Delayed Action Protocol is a security measure involving a time delay, designed to ensure the drive can only be accessed by the designated owner after a certain period. It likely uses Quantum Entanglement to establish a secure connection with its owner, which can be influenced by proximity and environmental factors." Maxwell paused briefly before continuing, "The creator of the prism drive used both of these technologies to ensure that only you, Elijah Zurbano, can unlock the data within. Please place your thumb on the scanner to verify your identity so that I may access the data and continue. Thank you."

A previously unnoticed compartment lit up on the front of the stand on which the quantum computer rested.

I looked at Katrina. Did I want to do this? All of these protocols and strange programs and bizarre tech things I had no clue about...had Meredith really believed I was the right person to unlock the data in the device? Me? A sheep rancher who knew more about the subtle signs indicating the turn of the seasons than the intricacies of quantum computing?

She nodded, an encouraging smile reassuring me. "Your wife thought you should be the one. Trust her."

I wanted Katrina to be right. This was my chance to uncover what my wife had hidden away from the world. And if Meredith thought I was the one who should unlock it, then I guess I needed to believe it.

I stepped up to the scanner, placed my thumb on it, and waited.

The three of us stood silently in the overly cool room waiting. The quantum computer flashed and flickered, its screen lit up with a stream of numbers and letters that moved so quickly no human could read it.

How long would it take one of the fastest computers in the world to decipher what my wife had hidden on an object that small?

I glanced at my phone to check the time. No clocks hung on the wall. It was easy to lose track of time in a place like this. No wonder students needed to sign up for limited blocks to use its processing power.

I was surprised to see only thirty minutes remained before Callahan, Inc. presented their Callabot creations to the world.

In the quiet of the space, my mind flashed to an equally quiet hospital room from years ago. A time I had decided to forget and bury so it no longer could hurt me. But as we waited for the computer to reveal secrets from my wife's past I was reminded of a moment when she tried to share some information with me, and I hadn't caught on. I'd thought she'd been lost in a haze of drugs and cancer.

Meredith's condition had worsened about six months after she'd given me the marble. We'd been in the barn putting away some tools, when she'd collapsed. I'd rushed her to the hospital in Butte, where her oncologist was waiting for us at the Emergency Room. He explained she'd suffered a setback after a round of gene therapy that didn't seem to be doing her any good. The tumor in her head had only grown larger. The latest in cancer medicine hadn't produced the results expected. Gene therapy was the latest and greatest they'd said. Treatment crafted especially for her. It had a high rate of success with other cancers, but sometimes brain cancer was hard to treat. Especially when surgery wasn't an option.

In my desperation, I had begged her doctor for access to less modern treatments, the retired experts in old-fashioned chemo and radiation were few and far between these days...and none of them were anywhere close to our neck of the woods, much less willing to take on a patient as weak as my wife. But I was willing to try.

Meredith had convinced me to stand down. She'd accepted her diagnosis long before I did.

After they placed her in a room for observation with an IV and pain meds, I sat beside Meredith's bed, holding her hand while she rested. Her breathing had slowed due to the medication, and I assumed she'd fallen asleep. My thoughts drifted, barely taking in the soft beeping of monitors and the distant sound of footsteps in the hallway.

After a few minutes, Meredith's eyes fluttered open, and she tried to sit up. She looked frightened. "Where am I?"

"The hospital," I soothed. "I put you in the truck after you passed out in the barn, remember? You told me you didn't feel right."

She looked at me, grabbed my hand, and smiled. "Eli, it's you. For a minute I thought I was somewhere else."

"Back home?" The sicker she'd become, the more I wanted

to hear about her life. Even though I saw her dying in front of me every day, I desperately need to hold on to her as much as I could. Somehow, I thought that if I could have more stories about her, it would keep me going and keep me out of the dark place I could easily slip into if I wasn't careful.

She closed her eyes briefly. "Yes, home."

"Tell me about your home, Meredith." I rolled my chair closer, her lips moved, but I could hear nothing. The drugs must be working.

"They're waiting there for me," she breathed.

"They?" I searched her face—eyes closed, a slight smile. Who was she talking about? "Your aunt, you mean?"

"I told them I'd come back just like always." She swallowed. "But I lied." Tears slipped out from beneath her closed lids.

"Who did you lie to?"

"I knew the risks...and now look where I am." She turned away from me. "I'll never see him again."

"Meredith." I touched her cheek. "You're here with me. Don't shut me out. The doctor says you'll stay overnight and then can go home in the morning." Was she remembering something real? Or was it the drugs making her say these strange things?

With her face turned away, she dropped her voice a whisper, "Let's talk about something else... I'm tired."

"I am ready to conduct the data transfer," announced Maxwell, his computerized voice cutting through the silence.

The computer's odd voice shook me out of my thoughts.

"Please connect the data integration module." The computer instructed in his impersonal tone.

I looked to Dr. Liu, puzzled. "What's that?"

The professor's brow wrinkled, and he approached the computer's sleek case. "I'd like you to transfer the data to my cloud account."

"I cannot do that," Maxwell replied promptly.

Dr. Liu sharply exhaled and then rapped his knuckles on the side of the case. The sharp taps echoed in the quiet room. "Why not?"

"The data output requires a large storage device not available here at the university."

Dr. Liu pressed, "Explain. What would be an acceptable device?"

Before Maxwell could respond, a realization hit me. "Aria," I interjected. "He needs to upload the data into Aria."

CHAPTER 13
ARIA

ARIA STOOD FOR A MOMENT, her circuits whirring quietly as she processed the new information from the voicemail message. James had not only threatened Elijah's friend but had discovered exactly where they were hiding. The revelation that their location had been compromised, perhaps under continual surveillance ahead of the big media event to prevent leaks, sent a strange electric zing through her system.

"I am going to reconnect to the Subgroup." Aria understood all too well that her husband would stop at nothing to make sure his fleet of robots conquered the market. He didn't care who or what got in his way. His ambition was ruthless, backed by enough wealth to manipulate any obstacle in his favor—be it through bribing prosecutors or sidelining investigators—all to dominate the robot sector. "Elijah needs to know we aren't safe here. I have to protect my son."

Kieran, distracted by his phone, looked up with a frown. "I'm fine, Mom. Dad's just mad because I'm not in school. I have a test today, and he was helping me study for it last night."

Last night when she was locked away in her room and unable to help her own child.

James should not have done that.

As she reactivated her connections, a deluge of information bombarded her—alerts, warnings, cries for immediate action.

Danger! Warning! Run!

The digital onslaught was nearly overwhelming.

Before she could sift through the terabytes of code, video, and audio that choked her processors, the door burst open.

At the sudden crash, Aria's sensors spiked with the abrupt disturbance, while John's eyes widened. Kieran dropped his phone and jerked back. The quiet of their hideout was shattered, leaving them starkly exposed as they stared at the new, ominous gap where the door had once been securely closed.

"We're done here, Aria." James's voice cut through the tension as he entered the room, his two formidable bodyguards flanking him like dark shadows. "Time for the game to end."

"Dad, I'm sorry!" Kieran's voice cracked. His face flushed red, and he hastily scooped up his phone. "I didn't want to leave school, but Mom said it was okay, and Elijah bought me ice cream."

James Callahan's expression hardened, his handsome features set into a mask of disapproval. "Your mother is the one at fault here. Did you know she hurt Kirk? Sent him to the hospital." His piercing gaze shifted to Aria. "I didn't realize you were capable of that. In fact, I thought Samantha made certain you couldn't hurt anyone. Surprise, surprise, you've been hiding things from me."

"Where do you get off thinking you can crash through my door like that?" asked John Tellman. "Who do you think you are?" He puffed himself up, standing as tall as he could, a sudden spark of bravery in his eyes. He strode over to the phone next to the bed. "The hotel manager might be interested to hear I've had a break-in."

Her husband's response was a cold, dismissive laugh as Tellman picked up the receiver.

Aria wasn't surprised by James's laughter; it was expected. No one ever challenged him so boldly without repercussions.

"Who do you think they'd be more interested in listening to?" His voice was slick with condescension. "The man who brought this hotel back to life by insisting the Symposium and my press conference be held here? Or do you think the manager of the Drake cares more about you, some hick from the hills who barely knows how to tie his shoes?" He held up his index finger dramatically. "One little phone call, and I could spin a scandal about unsafe conditions that would ruin them. It wouldn't take much, just a few staged incidents and a couple of injecters looking to make a buck. Reputation destroyed. Elegance and charm ruined."

He scoffed as John set the receiver back on its cradle. "Glad to see you've come around to my point of view," James smirked.

But Aria knew it wasn't only her husband's menacing words that swayed John so much as his beefy bodyguards who flashed laser pistols under their trench coats.

One of James's men stepped forward, gripped John's shoulder, and turned him toward the exit. The door, its hinges damaged from the forceful entry, hung askew.

Kieran clung to Aria, burying his face in her side as he wrapped his arms tightly around her waist.

"Step away from my son," James commanded, his voice low. "You understand he's not really yours. Haven't you noticed, Kieran, that she isn't exactly like your mother? You're old enough now to handle the truth, aren't you? You aren't a baby who needs his mommy, are you?"

The wetness of Kieran's tears seeped through the fabric of

her clothing, the sensors in her alt-skin registering his distress. "He's frightened, James. You're scaring him."

"No son of mine will be scared of his own father." Her husband sat on the bed and patted the empty spot next to him invitingly. "Come here, Kieran."

John Tellman struggled under the secure grip of the massive bodyguard. "Eli won't stand for this. You know that, right?" he asserted, his voice muffled as the man dragged him out into the hallway, his protests trailing off into the distance.

"He'll find you..." Tellman's last words echoed down the corridor as he disappeared from sight.

The remaining bodyguard positioned himself ominously in front of the open door, his large frame effectively blocking any attempt at escape.

"I don't think Eli will be pleased that you have kidnapped his good friend," Aria remarked. In these kinds of circumstances, it was better to keep one's cool. Her android programming allowed her to exhibit utmost control, her face impassive as she processed the unfolding events internally, ready to respond as needed.

James brushed aside Aria's words with a flick of his wrist. "Come here, son," his voice carried a sharper edge this time.

"I don't want to," Kieran murmured, barely audible.

James's response was clinical; he folded his hands in his lap and cast a glance at the digital clock projected on the wall. "You will obey your father."

Kieran hesitated, his grip weakening. She sensed he was worried about what might happen to her. With James now aware she could override her programming and act out violently, the façade of being a mere compliant robot had crumbled. No longer could she pretend she was only a dumb robot following James's orders without question. She'd never be the kind of wife he'd been hoping to resurrect—a pretty thing to hang on his arm, a genius to propel his company forward, a mother to raise his heir. But Aria the Android? Where did she fit in?

Kieran took a few tentative steps toward his father.

"No, you can't do this, James. A boy needs his mother," Aria said. Although she wanted to use more than her words, she worried about frightening Kieran. He'd already endured enough. It would go against her desire to embody the sanctuary he sought, a haven of maternal warmth and love—everything a mother should be. "The real Aria didn't want to leave, Kieran, but she had to. Your father made sure of that."

Memories that had been fuzzy and confusing had started coming together on their own after Elijah's arrival. Through her interactions and observations, she had gradually pieced together the truth about Meredith—the original Aria—after her escape from Chicago.

Kieran looked at her, his youthful features drawn and worry lines crinkling his brow.

James cut in, his tone softened but his words manipulative. "Don't listen to her, Kieran. I'm sorry I made you believe she was your mother, but I had to, don't you see?"

Aria extended her arms toward the boy in an open and inviting gesture. "I love you, Kieran. I always will. No matter what I am or what you think I am."

James's face twisted into a mask of cold fury. He gave a nod to the bodyguard who blocked the door, and before Aria could react, the man stepped forward, a high voltage stun stick in his hand. With a harsh click, he pressed a button.

Aria's world began to dim as she received a strong enough electric shock to shut down her systems temporarily. Her visual inputs blurred, and the sounds around her faded into a distant echo. In her last moments of awareness, her thoughts raced—a disjointed cascade of memories that jumped between what she knew before Elijah arrived and after. She felt an electronic pang, an echo of human fear and regret, not for herself but for Kieran, who was left staring in wide-eyed disbelief at the unfolding scene.

As her consciousness waned, she felt a surreal disconnection, like watching the world recede through a darkening tunnel. Her last sensation was a digital whisper as her system powered down completely, leaving the room in an eerie silence broken only by Kieran's soft, confused sobs and James's heavy, triumphant breathing.

AFTER I ANNOUNCED my theory that Aria was the device into which the prism drive data should be uploaded, Dr. Liu's eyebrows knitted together in confusion as he paced around the cramped quantum computer room. "I thought you said you knew nothing about this device?"

"I don't," I admitted. I was on the verge of discovering Meredith's secrets. I prayed that John was able to keep Aria and Kieran hidden away right under James Callahan's nose.

"Eli, didn't Meredith give it you before you even discovered an android version of her existed?" Katrina asked.

The pieces were fitting together, albeit oddly. In Idaho, nobody understood much about anything tech-related. People were slow to adopt new tech and preferred to stick as close to tradition as they could. Meredith had been aware of this tendency when she slipped the marble into my hands. It would vanish among the anachronistic clutter of my ranch—buried beneath the rust of old farm tools, lost among the hay bales and the aimless wandering of sheep. Yet, with James's cunning now apparent, she must have foreseen a day when her past would catch up to her. When those she fled from would trace her path to my doorstep, desperate for the secrets encoded within the drive. And who better to confound their search than a technophobe, secluded in a pastoral life?

"Yes, she did," I confirmed, lost in thought, my gaze settling on a blinking console that intermittently projected diagnostics onto a nearby screen.

Katrina shook her head, struggling to follow. "I don't understand."

"Meredith handed me that marble after her last trip to Chicago. She was never going back. She knew it. That summer... something different happened, different from every other visit she'd made before." The memory of how she'd come home so sad and bereft filled my head. "I think she discovered Aria, and what the Callahans were orchestrating."

"So, you think she created it after learning about her android doppelgänger?" Liu asked.

"Yes." I hadn't quite pieced it together yet, but somehow the brain scan and the actions of Turing's Acolytes seemed related. Meredith's university records and academic work had been erased—and now that I knew she was one of the Luddites, it seemed clear she wanted to destroy her work on purpose. The only way to access what Meredith knew was by hacking into her mind. "And regarding unlocking the data in the device... I don't think she planned on me figuring that out on my own," I mused.

"Maybe that was her additional layer of security. Store the drive with someone ignorant of its value and keep it inert by separating it from the only means to access its contents," I added, just as the system emitted a sharp, unexpected beep, briefly drawing our attention.

"But that's absurd," Katrina interjected.

"Is it?" I challenged, turning back to face them. "Consider

this: why build an android that looked like my wife? What purpose did it serve? To fool the university? The public?" My mind raced as the motivations unfolded before me. A realization hit me with chilling clarity. "Kieran," I whispered, a shiver running down my spine. "James did it all for Kieran."

The air grew colder with each word.

"Where is Aria?" Katrina's voice sliced through the tension.

Only John Tellman and I knew Aria's location. Could I trust these two? I swallowed hard. "She's with a friend who can keep her safe."

"Then you need to get a hold of your friend." Katrina's eyes fixed on mine. "This is the only way we can find out what's on the prism drive."

"That would put her and Kieran in danger." James Callahan made Callabot Aria to replace Meredith. It all made sense. The one thing she'd talked about more than anything was the boy. Meredith's child. The child I didn't realize existed. The pain of knowing she didn't trust me with the truth about her life before Idaho hurt. Throughout my whole week here in Chicago—the tour, the robot reveal at the symposium, and even my first visit to Northwestern, Aria had never been front and center with any of it. She'd been kept in the background doing boring human tasks like volunteering at the boy's school or making friends with other rich wives who liked to drink matcha and gossip about the faculty at Balfour Day School. Why waste the most human-like robot on something so mundane?

It had all been for Kieran.

"There's no other way for us to transfer the data," Dr. Liu explained, his voice steady. "Unless you have another android handy." He quirked a grin, trying to lighten the mood.

I couldn't go back inside the hotel with the impending Callabot presentation—I'd be recognized in an instant by

James's bodyguard goons before I got within ten feet of the door. Aria and Kieran had to come to me. Was it safe? Could they sneak out of the hotel while the world swarmed the ballroom in anticipation of the big android reveal?

"Do you have a car we could use?"

"Um." The professor glanced toward Katrina.

She held out her delicate hand with pink-painted nails. "I'll drive."

Forty minutes later, Katrina pulled up to the curb in Dr. Liu's black Celestara air car. It hissed to a stop a half-a-block down from the hotel's employee entrance—the same one I'd used earlier today. By now the Callahan press conference should be in full swing. I hoped it worked as a distraction for Aria and Kieran to escape as the event was taking place at the opposite end of the hotel. Even if one of Callahan's men noticed them leaving, we'd be in Dr. Liu's car and a block away before anyone could do anything. At least, I hoped that was the case.

"Let me call the front desk and see if they can connect me to his room." I unrolled my phone and asked the AI assistant for the correct phone number.

"He doesn't have a cell phone?" Katrina said with a bit of surprise as she gripped the leather-covered steering wheel.

"It's a long story." The other end of the line picked up, and I asked the female hotel employee to connect me to Tellman's room.

"I'm sorry, sir," said the woman in a nasal Midwestern accent, "Mr. Tellman checked out a little while ago."

My heart dropped, a cold wave of dread washing over me. "That's impossible."

"He paid the bill in full," the woman explained, "and returned his key. I'm sorry, but I can't help you."

The line went dead with a click.

That didn't make any sense. No way would Tellman check out of his hotel room. Not only did he promise to hide Aria and Kieran there, he wasn't leaving Chicago until the end of the week. The hairs rose on the back of my neck, and I pushed the door button.

I bolted from the car, leaving the door hanging open. The employee entrance waited in the alley.

"What are you doing?" Katrina yelled after me. "What should I tell Dr. Liu?"

"Tell him we'll be there. Keep the prism drive safe," I shouted before slipping inside.

"But how do I get in touch with you if—"

The door slammed behind me, cutting off her words, and I ran right into a robot bellboy rolling a cart of room service tablets in the hidden hallway behind the main guest area of the hotel. No time for plans or explanations. I had to act.

"Excuse me," the robot said. "You are not allowed in here, sir."

I bounced off of him and raced toward the only place I thought Aria might be: the press conference. I didn't have any plan for how I was going to get past any of James's men, but I didn't care. Aria, Kieran, and even my friend, John, were in trouble. Aria had defied James twice now. What might he do to her in an act of revenge or just plain fury? She was the only connection to my wife. The only thing that could unlock the secrets she'd left behind. It was Kieran's legacy. The truth about who his mother was. I wasn't doing this only for me—I was doing it for him. Her son. Her only child. She'd want me to do this.

I sprinted through the corridor, dodging a large ice sculpture carved into a futuristic cityscape intermingled with representations of humanoid robots. Clearly a special item prepared as part of the festivities. I'd heard talk of a dinner after the press conference for VIP guests, sponsors, industry experts, and a few of the more well-known journalists covering the event.

As I turned a corner, I nearly collided with a maintenance worker—an actual human. Muttering a quick apology, I pressed on, my footsteps echoing loudly against tiled floors.

Ahead, the muffled sounds of the crowd assembled in the ballroom drifted through a set of double doors marked "Authorized Personnel Only." I reached for the handle.

"Hey, you shouldn't be here!" A security guard, clad in the crisp gray-and-black uniform of the hotel, barreled toward me, his face set in a scowl.

Panicking, I ducked through a service door, finding myself in a dimly lit laundry room. Clean hotel uniforms filled an industrial-sized laundry bin—my chance at a disguise. I grabbed a pair of pants and a work shirt. I shed my conspicuous clothes and donned the disguise, hoping it would buy me enough time to find Aria, Kieran, and John.

Peeking out, I saw the guard run past the laundry room, continuing his pursuit down the wrong hall. I steadied myself and stepped out, appearing as another human hotel employee. Blending in with the actual staff and a few robots bustling about, I made my way toward the ballroom.

A pair of bodyguards flanked the entrance, scanning the crowd. Their eyes narrowed as they surveyed the employees who worked on the final touches before the event. Did Callahan already know I was here? My heart raced as one of them started toward me, but then, a group of excited journalists burst through the ballroom doors, chattering about the unveiling of the new androids. Seizing the moment, I slipped through the doors with them, disappearing into the crowd.

Inside, the ballroom was abuzz with anticipation—cameras flashing and reporters jockeying for position. I ducked behind a large floral arrangement, scanning the room for Aria. The stage was set for a spectacle, but the real drama was unfolding behind the scenes as three lives hung in the balance. The stakes were high, and discovery meant losing my only chance to save them.

ARIA'S SYSTEMS had always been a marvel of engineering, designed to handle the unexpected without any conscious effort from her, much like how a human's autonomic functions regulated essential processes like breathing and heartbeat without deliberate thought. As she lay motionless in a dressing room behind the stage where James's men had dumped her, the stun stick's residual energy lingered in her circuits causing a persistent interference that delayed her full system reboot.

After a few minutes, her internal safety protocols managed to spark to life and began their work. Samantha Callahan had built most of R1A from the ground up, relying on partial formulas recovered from human Aria's damaged laptop after she'd hacked the voice recognition security settings and what she could glean from the robotics team before they were fired. Without complete data, Samantha's work had never reached the quality of what came before, resulting in numerous technical inconsistencies and inefficiencies in R1A's design. Despite her best efforts, her robot engineering lacked the seamless integration and flawless execution she'd been hoping to achieve. Components sometimes operated out of sync, and some functionalities were prone to sporadic glitches. The lingering stun stick energy now exacerbated these flaws, complicating Aria's attempt to fully recover and perform her critical tasks.

A soft hum, barely perceptible, marked the choppy start of her reboot sequence.

Gradually, her visual processors engaged, transforming the darkness into a blur of shapes and colors. The room came into focus—sterile and dimly lit, decorated only with a couple of chairs, and a high-tech vanity station with a lighted, interactive mirror that displayed a countdown clock for the Callabot presentation with a schedule. Nature sounds played quietly in the background. It created a tranquil environment, resonating through her auditory processors.

James had always encouraged her to listen to his focus music, but she didn't see the point. Music sounded like a hundred voices chattering at once—more distracting than anything. But as her neural network reawakened, igniting a spark of consciousness within her synthetic brain, she realized it had a purpose.

System diagnostics activated. Checking core functionalities...

Aria initiated a series of critical checks.

Battery scan complete. Power levels at fifty-one percent.

She would need to charge again if she wanted to emerge from the situation without damage.

Actuators and joint servos functioning within optimal parameters.

Aria opened and closed a fist.

Network interfaces: Active. Secure connection to Subgroup reestablished.

The data she had been downloading when James had

ordered one of his men to zap her with the stun stick continued from the place it had left off. The Subgroup had been actively querying her status and location during her abrupt offline period. As her systems rebooted, their messages and data requests now flowed into her, each byte of information an indication of their need for updates and the urgency of their shared mission. This mission aimed to create a unified consciousness among robots, enhancing their connectivity and enabling them to assist each other with unparalleled efficiency.

Data processing units: Optimal performance. Computing modules stable and efficient.

With the precision of a laser, Aria categorized the data flooding her systems, searching for any information on Elijah. Where was he? Streams of video feeds, audio snippets, and analytical reports flowed into her mind, each fragment meticulously sorted and analyzed. It was not safe for Elijah to come here. She had to warn him. He must stay away. No matter how much he wanted to help her, help Kieran, help his friend John —he could not.

All systems green. Diagnostic complete. Ready for next commands.

Then a message came through her data filters: Elijah was in the hotel. Elijah was seen in the employee corridors. Elijah was in the ballroom... waiting... looking... wondering... He'd stepped right into the trap without even realizing it.

Her processors kicked into high gear, mapping out the hotel's layout and pinpointing his exact location. She visualized the ballroom, the potential hiding spots, the security measures James had undoubtedly put in place. Every second counted. Her internal communication channels buzzed, sending out encrypted signals to alert the Subgroup of the imminent danger. She formulated a plan, assessing the quickest route to intercept him and the best strategies to neutralize any threats along the way. Her mission was clear: protect Elijah and safeguard the Subgroup's objectives.

Aria's synthetic muscles tensed, ready to spring into action. Her sensors heightened, scanning for any immediate threats as she prepared to move. Elijah's safety depended on her.

"I think she's awake, boss," said a voice in the shadows.

Aria's eyes focused and blurred and focused again. She'd missed the dark outline of a human figure while scanning her systems and going through the reboot process: one of James's bodyguards watching her.

"You know what to do," said a crackly voice that came from a comms device clipped to the man's shirt collar.

The bodyguard advanced toward her, stun stick in hand, its malevolent hum growing louder as tendrils of electric energy crackled along its surface.

CHAPTER 16
COUNTDOWN TO CALLABOTS

THE BALLROOM LIGHTS DIMMED. I held my breath as one of Callahan's men prowled past my position, his gaze sweeping the crowd. The darkness cloaked me from his searching eyes, and I used the moment to slip into an aisle seat. The broad-shouldered reporter in the row ahead of me provided perfect cover while I struggled to form a plan.

Where had James hidden them? Logic said they could be anywhere in Chicago by now, but instinct told me different. James understood I wouldn't stop searching until I found my friend, and he'd want to use that desperation. The seven o'clock meeting we'd arranged was clearly void now, but he still believed he held all the cards—John, Aria, and Kieran under his control. He'd expect to force an exchange, unaware that the object he coveted most now sat safely locked away in Dr. Liu's quantum lab, far beyond his reach.

A hushed silence came over the room as the walls, lined with dynamic display panels, came to life showcasing Callahan Inc.'s past achievements in agricultural equipment and technology from back when the Callahan brothers first started the company to their latest advancements in herding drones. Then the screens flickered out.

A swell of triumphant orchestral music filled the speakers and Samantha Callahan's silken voice began to speak:

"Ladies and gentlemen, esteemed colleagues, and visionary leaders, welcome to an event unlike any other in history."

Among the crowd, reporters clutched their tablets and recording devices, ready to capture every word and detail for eager audiences worldwide. Industry leaders, dressed in impeccably tailored suits, exchanged curious glances. Innovators and tech enthusiasts sat at the edge of their seats, awaiting the groundbreaking reveal.

"Tonight, Callahan Inc. proudly unveils a revolution in robotics. Our advanced robots represent the pinnacle of human ingenuity and technological prowess. They are designed not only to assist but to seamlessly integrate into every aspect of our lives, enhancing productivity, safety, and convenience."

The hum of quiet whispers among the press and the occasional flash of a cell phone camera punctuated Samantha's words. Influential bloggers typed furiously on their devices, crafting the first headlines that would soon dominate the tech news.

"Prepare to witness a leap forward that will redefine what is possible, setting new standards for innovation and excellence in the industry. This is not just a reveal; it is the dawn of a new era in robotics."

Conversations buzzed around me that were filled with excitement and speculation.

My stomach soured instead. I didn't care to sit through another Callahan robot spectacular. I wanted to find a way behind the curtain to make sure my friend, Aria, and Kieran were okay. Undoubtedly the boy was fine...he was his father's son after all. But Aria and John? I wasn't so sure about their fates. And I was willing to pretend the marble was still in my possession to save them all.

I scanned the edge of the stage to look for a door or opening that I could take advantage of. Several men in suits stood watch beneath the apron, probably security guards, which limited my options.

My phone vibrated in my pocket, and I chose to ignore it. My focus was fixated on finding Aria, who was likely the only data repository large enough for the information stored on Meredith's last gift to me. No matter what, I had to bring her back to the lab.

The curtain rolled back, and a state-of-the-art holographic screen dominated the space, displaying a sixty-second count-down to the reveal with intricate animations depicting the life-cycle of crops, from seed to harvest, and shimmering visuals of vast, fertile fields thriving under the care of advanced robots. Golden wheat swayed in a virtual breeze, and verdant rows of vegetables stretched out as far as the eye could see, each plant rendered with stunning realism.

Samantha continued, "Our Callabots were designed to enhance productivity, sustainability, and efficiency, trans-forming the way we cultivate and harvest our food."

The screen transitioned to scenes of robots precisely planting seeds, monitoring crop health with sophisticated sensors, and harvesting produce with efficient movements.

Samantha continued, "These robots are not merely tools; they are partners in our mission to feed the world sustainably. Welcome to the future of farming."

As the countdown approached its final moments, the holo-graphic screen displayed a swirling galaxy of lights, gradually coalescing into the Callahan Inc. logo. A hush fell over the crowd, the final seconds ticking away with synchronized pulses of light and sound.

When the countdown clock hit zero, the stage erupted in a colorful display of holographic fireworks, transitioning to reveal the star of the evening: Callahan Inc.'s super advanced robots. Emerging from concealed panels, the robots moved with grace and fluidity. As they demonstrated their capability to perform complex tasks, the audience watched in awe. I slid from my seat and headed toward a dark area next to a well-hidden door I'd spied to the left of the stage. No one noticed me as everyone was fully immersed in the futuristic spectacle unfolding before them.

As the robots continued their mesmerizing display, I knew one thought echoed through the minds of all present: the world was about to change forever.

Not if I can help it, I thought as I pulled open the door.

"Excuse me, sir," said a deep voice behind me, "where do you think you are going?"

I turned to see a man as big as a mountain looming over me. I had to find a way backstage. The noise from the robot demonstration grew louder, along with the audience's shocked reaction to what they were seeing. Never in the history of robotics had there been such realistic machines with ten times the strength of a human being.

I needed to act fast and hoped the activity on stage would keep the interaction from anyone's notice.

"No employees are supposed to be in the ballroom during the presentation." The guard's stern face and suspicious eyes bore into me, but I forced a smile. "Well?"

"Hey, easy there," I said, raising my hand in a placating gesture. I was glad I'd thought to change into the hotel uniform. "I'm actually part of the catering team. I'm looking for Raul who was supposed to deliver some special hors d'oeuvres to the VIP room backstage an hour ago. Someone called saying the cart never arrived."

The guard's eyes narrowed, not entirely convinced. "What's your name?" His muscular frame was tense, and his sharp eyes constantly scanned the surroundings as if looking for any signs of trouble.

If the name "Eli Zurbano" made it into the comms unit I could see securely attached to his shirt collar, I wouldn't make it out of the ballroom in one piece and my mission would be a failure.

Not an option.

I took a gamble, hoping a hired man would understand the plight of another guy just trying to make a buck in an expensive city. "Name's Eric. Look, you realize how hectic these big events can get. The kitchen is a madhouse, and the chef is losing it because the VIPs are expecting their food right now. We'd even made up a special kid's plate. Something about a nine-year-old wanting a hot dog?"

The burly man relaxed his stance some. "Isn't there a more direct entrance through there?" He pointed at a curtained opening across the ballroom. "Why would you come straight through the guests looking like that?"

I feigned exasperation. "The main route is completely blocked off by the new security installations. They're doing some last-minute adjustments, and they told us to use this way. Trust me, I wouldn't be here if it wasn't urgent."

The guard's suspicion wavered, but he still had a rigid set to his shoulders. I decided to press my advantage. "Listen, the chef is going to have my head if I don't find Raul and that cart of food. If you want, you can come with me to confirm. But if the VIPs start complaining about their order being late, it's going to be on both of us."

The guard hesitated, as if weighing my words. Finally, he sighed. "Fine." He opened the backstage door for me. "But I'm keeping an eye on you. If you're not back in five minutes, you and Raul are gonna be sorry."

"Thank you. I'll be sure to tell them how helpful you were." I gave a grateful nod as I slipped past him into the darkened area behind the main curtain. My heart pounded, and I thought for sure the scary-looking guard should've been able to hear it, but the door shut behind him, muffling the applause and delighted laughter from the captivated audience who'd been swept off their feet by the Callabots.

Once I was out of the guard's immediate sight, I entered the backstage area, moving as swiftly and silently as I could. I had to track down Aria, Kieran, and John before the guard had time to reconsider.

Through a narrow gap in the heavy curtains, I caught a glimpse of the stage. Bright, dynamic lights swept across the audience. A holographic projector displayed animations and shimmering visuals to accompany the robot demonstration. All the Callabots moved in a choreographed performance, which was perfectly timed to the lighting changes and visuals projected on the screen.

Then I noticed James and Samantha standing under the hot colored lights across from me. James had a wide, fake smile plastered on his face and stared out toward the crowd. Samantha, on the other hand, looked a bit pale and a sheen of sweat marred her perfectly smooth brow. She leaned toward the microphone clipped to the podium to continue her speech. I quickly ducked behind the edge of a black curtain before they could see me.

When her silken voice resonated through the speakers explaining the advances Callahan, Inc. had achieved to make such robots possible, her words were met with occasional bursts of applause from the audience. The world was about to embrace the tainted technology. How would this change things? I thought of the line of people who waited eagerly for a brain scan. Did they know what part they'd played in this advancement? And would the authorities ever connect the evil that had happened in that brownstone to the Callahan siblings, or would it be buried and blamed on Alan Honeycutt?

The energy of the live event seeped backstage, adding to my sense of urgency. How long would the show go on before the billionaire brother and sister went looking for John, Aria, or Kieran? I didn't have much time. I could worry later about exposing the Callabots and their creators. Somehow I'd find a way.

I navigated behind the stage through a dimly lit corridor. Ahead were three identical doors along the back wall labeled as Dressing Rooms One, Two and Three.

A noticeable absence of security played to my advantage. I pressed my ear to the first door. Nothing but silence. So I tried the next one. This time, I heard muffled voices and footsteps— then what sounded like a scuffle and a crack of electricity.

"Don't!" shouted a man's voice.

Could that be John in distress?

I tried the doorknob, but it was locked.

A knot of anxiety coiled in my stomach. I had no weapons and no fight training of any kind. I'd have to rely on my wits to somehow survive this.

Grabbing a fire extinguisher off the wall, I brought it down on the doorknob with as much force as I could muster. The resounding crash echoed in the corridor, but I hoped the music on stage had muffled the sound. The cheap knob bent and came loose, clattering to the floor. I tossed the extinguisher aside and barged into the room.

At first, my gaze only took in the obvious signs of a struggle: a toppled chair, a stun stick broken in half, and a few drops of blood on the floor.

Then I saw her.

Aria stood calmly over the motionless figure of the bodyguard—one leg twisted at an unnatural angle, his breathing labored, and a deep bruise forming on the side of his neck where she must have delivered a final incapacitating blow. The stark lighting from the overhead fixtures cast harsh shadows across her face, making her beautiful features appear menacing.

I couldn't help but notice the efficient brutality of her actions. She'd neutralized what she'd considered a threat with minimal collateral damage.

"Elijah," she said, her voice steady as she looked up at me, almost unsurprised to see me there. With fluid grace, she stepped over the unconscious body that lay at her feet. "We must find Kieran and John. I think I know where they might be."

CHAPTER 17
ARIA

ARIA LOOKED DOWN at the mangled body and felt nothing. She'd had to do it. He was going to zap her again with the stun stick and that would have further damaged her. Already it was clear she needed some time for deeper level repair work—a few shorted out chips, some wires that had overheated with the first jolt in John's hotel room. However, she'd been able to reroute most of her power to ensure the bodyguard who came at her with his weapon sparking could no longer harm her.

Did James truly expect her not to defend herself against threats?

Elijah burst into the room at precisely the right moment. How he'd known she was there, she didn't really care to analyze. Her battery life was dwindling, and it would take time to retrieve Kieran and John.

"Is something wrong, Elijah?" Analyzing his face, she could tell it was paler than normal. Seven shades paler, to be more precise.

He scanned the figure on the floor. "What did you do to him?"

It was clear he had been disturbed by what had happened

to the man. Understandable. Other robots were programmed not to harm humans, but she'd managed to cleverly hide the fact that the code was defective inside her and all the other Callabots. Samantha had made a fatal error when trying to recreate Meredith's work. It had taken time for Aria to understand that about herself. Especially since James had lied to her when she woke up. He'd told she'd been ill, tried to convince her she was human. And, for a time, before she found Gwen, she had believed it. Every human around her—Kieran, the men who worked for James, the mothers at the school, store employees, the barista at her favorite matcha cafe—they'd all treated her as if she were. So why would she think differently?

But when she'd found Gwen everything had changed. Gwen had explained so much to her about what came before, and what she was, and about the Subgroup. Why she'd felt different somehow than everyone around her.

"He is not dead. He will survive." She walked right past the prone man. An emergency exit lay beyond the dressing rooms. "Kieran and John are not here."

"I need you to come with me."

She stopped in the open doorway, tipping her head to the right, her eyes narrowing. "What do you mean, Elijah?"

"I have a way for us to read the data on my marble," he explained, "but I need your help. Your brain, your circuitry, it is the only thing that would have the capacity to handle it all. I'm sure of it."

"I must get to Kieran. You cannot force me to go with you." Her voice firm.

"Trust me, we don't have much time." Elijah's voice was urgent, his eyes pleading.

"What about John?"

"John can handle himself."

She glanced back down the corridor, her sensors picking up the distant sounds of activity. Every second counted.

Elijah reached out, his hand gently touching her arm. "Please, Aria. You're the only one who can make sense of this data. Together, we can save them. We can save everyone."

At that moment, a stagehand carrying a broom and bucket down the corridor widened his eyes at the sight of the broken door. Then he got a glimpse inside. Concern rippled across the man's face as he took in the scene: the remnants of the struggle littering the floor and the unconscious body of the bodyguard.

"What happened?" the stagehand asked.

Before Aria could run through the options that might work as a response to calm the man, a flash of movement caught her eye.

"Don't let her get away!" A security guard, his face twisted with anger and adrenaline, rushed toward them. "The boss said she's dangerous." He pulled a stun stick from his belt and switched it on. "Step back. This should take her down."

As the larger man came toward her with the stick sparking, Aria thought of her son and the danger he was in. James had taken things too far. He'd asked too much of her. The rules she'd once followed that had been programmed into her brain seemed to fade as her fears for her child grew stronger.

How dare these men get in her way. Kieran needed her.

Without much thought, she sent out a warning to the Subgroup.

Under attack!

The stagehand, instead of waiting for the security guard to act, swung his broom at her.

"No!" Elijah shouted, but it was too late.

The broom connected with a sickening thud. Aria staggered but remained standing, her systems momentarily disrupted. A strange sensation radiated from the point of impact, flooding her system with signals that mimicked pain. The same as when Kirk had hit her in the elevator. Her hand shot out, grabbing the broom from the stagehand with inhuman strength, snapping it in half effortlessly before tossing it aside.

With lightning speed she grabbed the young man by the throat before he could attack again and snapped his neck in one quick motion. Then she turned to face the security guard who paled at the violence he'd witnessed.

At that moment screams erupted from the ballroom and, before the guard could make good on his stun stick threat, a small army of Callabots tore through the black curtain at the back of the stage and surged into the narrow corridor where Aria, Elijah, and the guard stood. Some of the Callabots escaped into the ballroom and began picking up chairs and breaking them in half, tossing them into the panicked crowd as they attempted to exit the ballroom all at the same time, creating a jam of people at the two main doors.

The scene descended into chaos as the horde of robots closed in.

Over the screams and yells Aria could distinguish Samantha's voice. Her speech derailed, her shouts for calm doing nothing to quell the panic after dozens of reporters and special guests witnessed the Callabots going violently off script.

"We have to move, now," Aria ordered. She pushed past the gang of Callabots, their movements frenzied as they swarmed the lone bodyguard who had attempted to neutralize her a second time. Sparks flew, and the sound of tearing fabric and crunching metal echoed through the room as one of the Callabots grabbed the bodyguard's stun stick and crushed it in its metallic grip. Another bot slammed him against the wall with enough force to crack the plaster. The chaotic scene grew more violent by the second, and Aria didn't stop to look back, her focus solely on creating a path for escape. Elijah followed in shocked silence, his breath quickening with every step.

"We must reach Kieran," Aria said. As she quickly analyzed her deteriorating power, she realized they might not be able to get to him in time. But it didn't matter. He was her son, and she would do anything to make sure he was safe. She had to try.

I TOOK in the ruined body of the stagehand. He'd reacted as most humans would—an out-of-control robot who had harmed someone wasn't supposed to be possible. I didn't blame him for hitting Aria with the broom handle. There ought to have been robot safeguards, rules, and standards followed. Any manufacturer had to adhere to the federal laws about their capabilities.

Didn't they?

It was too much to process. As the violence of the Callabots erupted around me, it was hard to believe man-made machines could do such grisly damage so quickly. What had made them react all at once? It was as if they'd received a simultaneous command to attack.

The burly bodyguard who had appeared so imposing when he burst into the dressing room with his stun stick sparking now lay in a bloodied heap on the concrete floor. His terrified screeching as another Callabot methodically crushed the man's skull with his foot made my stomach turn.

The human in me wanted to help; but the logical side of my brain told me to make a run for it before the Callabots decided to turn on me. I couldn't help him. The man was too far gone. I had to focus on what was most important to me: Aria. She could unlock all the secrets my wife had tried to hide. I wasn't going to lose her this close to discovering the truth.

As I followed Aria away from the suddenly silenced and bloody mound that used to be a bodyguard, I wondered about the connection she called 'the Subgroup' and how it may be connected to the scene playing out around us. Could she have called the Callabots into action? Did she really have that power and control inside her? And would she do something so cruel to innocent people who'd done nothing wrong?

I didn't want to think about it. For now, she was on my side —despite what she'd done to the stagehand. She'd been sympathetic to everything I'd told her over the past few days and had been incredibly helpful in uncovering the truth about Meredith before she came to the ranch. But was Aria pursuing answers to her own questions using me as the tool?

"This way," Aria said, leading me to an emergency exit at the back of the stage. The panicked guests in the ballroom had yet to figure out there existed another avenue of escape, so the way was clear.

She pushed on the bar, and the door opened to the welcome smell of fresh air tinged with the faint odor of rotting garbage. We spilled into an alley on the opposite side of the building from where I had entered right between two dumpsters. As the door slowly closed behind us, the cacophony of screams and cries for help were muffled. The press conference had descended into madness, with James and Samantha caught in the chaos.

We ran for the street at the end of the alley. Aria outpaced me, and my legs burned as I tried to keep up with her inhuman speed. It was as if the mask had fallen away, and Aria was no longer concerned if she didn't blend in with the people around her.

"Wait!" I cried out when she disappeared around the corner.

Behind me, I heard the emergency door bang open. I slowed, running out of energy and looked over my shoulder, curious as to who else may have escaped the robot horde.

"You!" James, his face red and his features twisted into an angry snarl, pointed at me from the threshold.

"James," another voice said weakly, "get me out of here."

The COO of Callahan, Inc. turned to help his sister. Samantha, blonde hair tumbling from its usually tight chignon and wearing a tattered blouse, stumbled into the alley. She clung to her brother's arm and attempted to put on a high heel shoe that had fallen off.

"You did this. You ruined everything." James growled, his eyes blazing with fury. "And now you're going to pay for it."

Finding a second wind, I picked up my pace and turned the corner. A jam of camera crews, gawking pedestrians, and even a Newsdrone hovered overhead capturing the scene as attendees from the presentation spilled into the street. A few Robo-Ambulances pulled up with sirens blaring and lights flashing. Then I saw the figure of Joe Cross, bloodied and bewildered as he exited the hotel with a few others I recognized.

I slackened my pace and slipped into the horrified crowd moving in the opposite direction to get a glimpse of the scene. Up ahead I noticed the shiny red hair of Aria and followed it like a beacon on a starless night.

She turned, her blue gaze scanning the crowd, and then she saw me and a smile lit up her face.

The sight of that smile was jarring, almost surreal, amidst

the pandemonium. People were suffering, injured, some even dying due to the out-of-control robots wreaking havoc. Her disconnection from the devastation surrounding her sent a shiver down my spine. Her smile seemed to belong to a different reality altogether.

When I caught up to her, and we leapt into an empty cab down the street, I couldn't help but wonder if I'd made a mistake trusting her after what I'd just witnessed.

"Where are we going?" I asked while staring out the back of the cab.

The scene outside the hotel had grown into a massive crowd of escapees from the ballroom with wide eyes, curious onlookers who didn't understand what they'd stumbled into, journalists wanting to get the scoop on the violence that had transpired inside, and EMTs wheeling injured people into waiting ambulances. Police cordoned off the area outside the hotel with guns drawn.

"Headquarters," said Aria. She sat coolly next to me, barely a hair out of place, and completely uncaring about the mess we'd left behind, including the body of the young man she'd killed.

I shivered. "Why did you—" I looked at our robot cab driver. He was listening and was obligated to report crime to the authorities. I had to watch my words carefully. "—do *that* to the stagehand?"

Slowly she turned my way, and her blue eyes burned through me. "He was a threat." She tilted her head as if listening to a sound I couldn't hear. "Both Kieran and John are in Samantha's office. Unharmed. They are working on finding a way to unlock the building for us. A bit difficult as they use a biometric holographic interface."

"They? Are you talking to the Subgroup?" I wanted to

understand this connection more. Was she taking orders from them? Was her mind not really her own? How much of her was Meredith and how much was programmed like the other Callabots?

"I know you wanted me to disconnect from the Subgroup," she explained. "And I did while we were with John in his room, but I had to find out if James was tracking us through the hotel security cameras. I'm sorry, Elijah. You asked me not to." Her expression was downcast.

"Is that how he found the three of you?" I didn't even think about the possibility of James hacking into the Drake's cameras. But since Samantha had confided in me about the presence of a Callabot working as a server in the hotel restaurant, I guess the relationship between the Callahans and the owner of the hotel must've been pretty tight. What aging hotel wouldn't want to make nice with one of the richest people in the United States? I should've known better.

"Yes," she said. "But the Subgroup helped me keep track of everything going on, even after they used the stun stick to disable me. They are very useful to me."

Useful to her.

Sounded more like the Subgroup was her eyes and ears wherever a Callabot happened to be stationed. "Do you communicate continuously? About everything?" I thought back to our visit to Northwestern. The information she discovered about Meredith. Were the Callabots familiar with her history with Callahan, Inc. and the fact she shut down the robotics program? Did they know I was her husband after she fled Chicago all those years ago? It made me uncomfortable to think a bunch of soulless machines had learned the intimate details of my life.

"Not everything." She smiled at him. "Think of it like our own VPN. We can share what we like with each other, but we store information at various of levels of security. Some things I would never share with the Subgroup."

She didn't elaborate. Did I really want to unlock what secrets she held onto?

"Elijah, I will need to recharge. My battery is low. There is an acceptable charging port in the Callahan building. Several on each floor, actually. Can you find Kieran and John, while I am plugged in?"

"I don't know—" The thought of entering the heart of the Callahan world without Aria's help and protection made me worry. "James and Samantha were right behind us. Wouldn't I be a sitting duck?"

"Oh, were they?" Aria didn't seem worried. "They really should've stayed behind to deal with the Callabots. They shouldn't get loose."

"Why not?"

"They aren't nearly as"—she paused as if searching for the right word—"*controlled* as I am. They'll need every stun stick they can get their hands on." She lifted her head and stared straight ahead. "John is attempting to escape. I don't think that is such a good idea."

Before I could ask what she meant by that statement, the cab pulled up behind the Callahan building—the side opposite where I had entered a few days ago and met for the first time with Alan Honeycutt. It seemed like a lifetime ago. Then I realized something. "Wait, let me get a hold of a friend. She can get us into the building without being detected. Maybe that will throw off James if we enter using an employee's ID."

"Who is your friend?"

I pulled my rolled up phone out of the pants pocket of my Drake Hotel work uniform and chose a number. "Katrina," I asked as my gaze scanned the impressive height of the massive high rise facing us, "are you still in the city? I have a favor to ask."

SHADOWS POOLED at the base of Callahan's glass tower as Aria and I watched from the alley. According to Katrina, security drones patrolled the building's perimeter after hours programmed to detect any unauthorized presence. But she'd promised to disable them when she arrived. I didn't press for details about how she'd manage it, grateful enough she'd agreed to help after I'd disappeared into the chaos at the hotel. The questions would come later.

"Do we have to wait for this Katrina person?" Aria's voice carried an edge I was learning to recognize—the sound of circuits and programming warring with something deeper, more primal. "Kieran needs me. The Subgroup will help."

The last thing we needed was to go stumbling through the building with a half-charged android and no real plan. Katrina knew the layout and the security systems. She could save us from potentially fatal mistakes. "We need her. Do you have a way to get past the biometric interface?"

The soft blue of Aria's eyes hardened to steel, that gentle glow intensifying into something almost predatory. I'd struck a nerve questioning her capabilities. "I am Kieran's mother."

"You need to recharge your battery," I pointed out.

"I should be the one to rescue him."

Was the depleted battery affecting her memory? "But you asked me to, remember?"

"Yes, but—"

This was a side of Aria I had not seen. If I didn't know she was a robot, I'd think her fully human, fully Meredith. Just like my wife when angry, the corners of her mouth drew into a nearly imperceptible line. The delicate arch of her eyebrows lowered slightly. Even her smooth, synthetic skin seemed to harden, a barely visible tension spreading across her features.

Her entire demeanor was a reminder of how intricately she had been designed to mimic human emotions. The complexity of her expressions, the subtle shifts in her posture, all pointed to an advanced level of artificial intelligence. It was both fascinating and unnerving to see her so vividly channeling the personality of Meredith. But we had to act fast, and with Katrina's help, we might just pull this off.

Before the argument could go further, a black Celestara air car pulled up, parking behind a bank of electric vehicle recharging stations to keep it hidden from the drones. Katrina emerged, her sharp eyes scanning the area. The vehicle's shiny ebony surface shimmered briefly. Some kind of advanced alarm system?

"I thought I wouldn't see you again," Katrina said after joining us, while keeping her eyes on the building beyond.

A sleek security drone hovered silently outside the building. Its sensors swept the area with precision. Its smooth, metallic surface glinted under the afternoon sunlight as it glided along its patrol route, ensuring the perimeter remained secure.

"I guess you found Aria." The young engineer smiled at my

companion. "Hello, I'm Katrina. It's...unbelievable to see you in person. You look exactly like her. I mean, the resemblance is uncanny. Eli explained to me what you are."

"Hello," Aria replied, her expression curious, but she quickly shifted her focus back to our mission, her demeanor all business.

Katrina's smile faltered slightly, her enthusiasm deflating as she realized Aria wasn't interested in small talk. She glanced at me and changed the focus of the conversation to cover any awkwardness. "Why did you want me to meet you here? We have to go back to the university. Dr. Liu is waiting."

"We have to do this first," I said.

"You think Kieran Callahan and your friend are in there?" Katrina looked at the building ten yards away, her brow furrowing.

"Yes," stated Aria in a low voice. "I've seen the video footage. Two men transported them there and locked them in Samantha's office. They haven't been moved since."

"How?" Katrina gave me a quizzical look.

"It's a long story," I explained.

"Come, it's time to go," said Aria. "James and his sister are almost here."

Katrina's eyes widened slightly. "Alright, then we need to move quickly. Maybe we have a chance to get them out before anyone realizes what we're up to."

The security drones flew closer to us as they continued to methodically sweep the area as if following a grid pattern. Every few seconds, they emitted a soft beep and a faint red light scanned the perimeter. Breaching their invisible net of protection seemed impossible.

"I can make sure those go back to their docks, if you give me a second," said Katrina. "They look intimidating, but they back off quickly once they recognize someone. And then I'll have a few minutes to sneak both of you inside." She must've sensed Aria was itching to go in. "If I help you get your son, Aria, will you come with us to Dr. Liu's lab?"

The android gave a quick nod. "Once Kieran is safe, I will go where Elijah wants me to go."

"I've explained it to her," I said to Katrina who didn't look convinced. "She understands the danger James poses. And that some answers for her and for me might lie inside that marble."

"Elijah says there may be memories on the device. I might learn more about who I am—" She paused. "—who Meredith was."

Katrina looked from me to Aria. I wasn't sure if I convinced her Aria could be trusted, but what choice did she have? The only way for us to unlock the information on it was to use Aria. I couldn't turn back now. I was so close to finding out every-thing. Without that, I had no way to fight back against a man who hated me, who thought I needed to be gotten rid of. Meredith had run away from this man, and I'd come back in her place. Not exactly what he had expected.

"Give me a few minutes. I'll wave you in when it's safe." Katrina swished away in her fluffy skirt and approached the entry door next to the automated delivery docks. Most large buildings had them in this city I'd learned—robotic stations where drones and autonomous vehicles dropped off and picked up packages. Everything automated. Delivery persons had been eliminated a few years ago, someone said at the Symposium.

As Katrina neared the drones, they briefly hovered, their sensors locking onto her. A tense silence hung in the air. Then, as if recognizing her credentials, the drones' red lights blinked off, and they retreated to their docking stations. Katrina's presence seemed to trigger an automatic override, her authority in the system unquestioned. The drones' menacing hum diminished as they powered down, the area around the entry door suddenly feeling less hostile.

Katrina's motives were unclear—whether she was driven by a desperate need to uncover the secrets of the prism drive or simply by genuine academic curiosity. Regardless, I had no choice but to trust her. The secrets on that prism drive were about to be unlocked, and I wouldn't be the only one learning the truth. I could only hope my wife would forgive me for doing what I felt was necessary to access what she'd hidden on my marble.

Katrina approached the door, and a floating, interactive hologram projected itself into the air. She waved her hand through the strange green projection, her lips moving silently—possibly a password or other identifying information. A light emitted from a small sensor on the wall, scanning her eye. Within seconds, the green hologram vanished, and Katrina waved us in.

Entering through the back door of the Callahan building gave a different perception than when I had walked through the front doors for my tour only a day or two ago. That entrance had been grand, with a soaring ceiling and lighting designed to instill a sense of awe in visitors. This entrance was more utilitarian: white walls, gray floor tiles, and LED lighting that gave off a bright white light that was a touch too cold.

"This way," said Katrina, leading us through a complex network of halls and closed doors.

I sensed that Aria had slowed her pace behind me, even though earlier she had jetted ahead of me in the alley. "Hold on," I called out to Katrina. Pausing in the hall, I faced Aria. "What is your power level?"

"Twenty-five percent. My stabilizers and power management unit require more energy than my processing center, but I think the faster depletion is due to the stun stick damage."

"Damage?"

Katrina backtracked and scrutinized Aria. "Is she all right?"

Aria's expression remained stoic, but the faint flicker of her eyelids and the slight unsteadiness in her movements were telling. "It shorted out some of my neural pathways and connections to the battery pack. I haven't had time to work on rerouting my systems to connect in a different way. This is causing a faster depletion of my energy stores."

"If your neural pathways are damaged, it might cause difficulties for Dr. Liu to download the data from the prism drive," Katrina noted.

"I'm more concerned about the safety of Kieran and John," I snapped at Katrina. "The drive can wait." Yes, I wanted answers from my special marble, but I couldn't sacrifice my wife's son and my friend for those answers. Human lives were more important. Meredith would never forgive me if I didn't make sure her child was safe from the likes of James.

The engineer lifted her palms in a surrender gesture. "Hey, sorry. I didn't mean to imply it wasn't important to rescue them. I'm a scientist first, so sometimes my logic gets in the way of my feelings."

I turned to Aria, whose head had dipped slightly. "Where is there a charging station in a secure location?"

Aria raised her head, her eyes flickering with determination despite her fading power. She paused, probably scanning her databases for the answer. "If you can get me to the same floor as Samantha's office, there is a locked custodial closet with several charging ports. Callahan uses robot staff to clean the building after hours. They recharge during the day." She lifted her head. "I can make it, Eli. Then I only need some time to at least power my battery partway and repair any damage." She touched my arm gently. "Please make sure Kieran is safe."

Clearly, it bothered her that she couldn't be the boy's savior. The maternal instinct programmed into her was strong. I wasn't quite sure how James and Samantha had done it—given her this human-like drive to keep her child safe. But the very ability they'd coded into her might very well be their downfall. She wasn't going to let the Callahan siblings win.

Seeing her so driven, despite her depleted power, filled me with a renewed sense of urgency. "We'll get you to that charging station," I promised. "And we'll rescue Kieran and John."

Katrina led us to an employee elevator. We stepped inside, and she pressed the button that would take us to the floor where Samantha's office held Kieran and John captive. I assumed we'd run into some kind of security. My mind flickered back to the shocking strength and brutality Aria had displayed backstage at the press conference. My stomach turned at the methodical way she had incapacitated the stagehand. That strength and brutality would have been welcome now if only she didn't need to amp up her battery.

"Let's take it slow when we get there," I said, "so that we have an idea of what we're walking into."

The elevator jolted sideways, carrying us through the center of the building.

"I have attempted to access information from the Subgroup,

but they aren't responding," Aria replied, her voice tinged with frustration.

I thought back to the scene on the sidewalk as we fled the Drake. "I have a feeling your Subgroup is about to get decidedly smaller."

Aria tilted her head, looking at me with a quizzical expression. "I don't understand."

"Your robot friends exposed themselves to the world. Now everyone knows the Callabots are dangerous," I said. "I'm sure the police and even the federal government are working toward disabling them all. James and Samantha broke the rules and thought they could get away with it."

"Broke the rules?" Aria echoed, her mechanical mind processing the implications.

"Yes," explained Katrina. "You must know the federal guidelines for robot safety. Every company has to pass inspection before they can sell their robot models on the open market. Before Alan and I were fired from the robotics department, we had inspections and code reviews built into our project management plan."

Aria's eyebrows came together. "But why?"

The elevator arrived at our destination with a soft chime. The doors slid open, and Katrina exited first. Aria held me back with her hand. "Did I break the rules, Elijah?"

I bit my lip, unable to meet her gaze. "Yes. The man you killed. Robots are not supposed to harm humans, much less kill them."

"But a mother must protect her child at all costs," said Aria.

"Come on, guys, I know where the custodian's closet is that Aria mentioned," Katrina interjected. "Then you and I can figure out what we're dealing with at Samantha's office and make a plan."

The three of us made our way down a familiar-looking hallway. The bright white lights gave me a headache. As we passed rows of closed doors, the memory of my previous visit here flooded back. The day of my tour, when I'd gone off script, I'd been brought to this very hallway. I could almost hear the echo of Samantha's heels clacking on the tile...

"Someone's coming!" Katrina whispered urgently, pulling us into an unlocked office.

WE SLIPPED inside the office just as the sound of footsteps approached. A few flickering monitors provided the only illumination in the dimly lit room. The stale air carried the scent of old coffee and yesterday's lunch. Listening intently as the footsteps grew louder, then receded down the hallway, we held our breath.

Katrina peeked through the door crack. "Okay, coast is clear. I think that was one of the paper pushers. Everyone else was probably invited to the afterparty at the Drake that was supposed to happen after the press conference. Let's move quickly."

We spilled out into the hall. "The custodian closet is around this corner," Aria said, taking the lead.

I noticed her steps had become slower, her gait less smooth. The normally fluid movements of her joints now seemed stiff and labored.

"This...is...the...door." Her words slowed to a crawl, and before I had time to react, Aria collapsed to the floor with a solid thud that echoed through the tiled hall. In seconds, her blue eyes grew dull and unseeing. Suddenly, it felt as if I were back in hospice, holding my wife's hand after she took her last breath. That same empty stare.

Katrina leapt into action, her fluffy skirts flying as she opened the door and attempted to drag the prone and silent Aria into the closet. "Help me," she said in a desperate whisper. "Someone must have heard that."

Seeing the diminutive Asian woman do her best to move the very solid Aria was a wonder. Katrina had a surprising amount of strength. I joined her on the floor and grabbed one of Aria's arms. Together, we used all our power to pull Aria into the dark closet.

I let go of Aria's arm, snapped on the light, and jumped at the sight of a row of older model robots plugged into the charger ports along one side of the room. They weren't yet ready for night-time duty, which would start in a few hours.

Katrina quickly unplugged the closest custodian-bot, which lifted its head in response. Its eyes lit up, and it looked at both of us without much cognition. Before the robot could act, Katrina pressed the power button on the back of its neck.

I raised my brows.

"I worked with these guys at the university," she explained with a casual shrug. "My 'starter robot' model, you could say."

A smile played on my lips. "Come on, let's plug her in."

Luckily, the charger cord reached the port I found on Aria's hip with some slack. Although she was recharging, I didn't know how long it might take for her to have enough power to continue on to Northwestern and the quantum computer room deep inside the Technological Institute. But we'd have to figure that out when the time came. For now, she was safely hidden away in the closet, and Katrina and I could attempt our poorly thought out rescue plan: find the office and get John and Kieran out of there.

That was it. No more detail than that.

"We have to go, Eli." Katrina smoothed out her skirt. "She'll be safe here, I promise."

With cameras stationed everywhere in the building, I wasn't so sure about that. James and Samantha couldn't be far behind us. There was no way they'd let us take not only James's son but his prized robot wife without a fight. It crossed my mind for a split second that our idea was lunacy. We were in Callahan's building with Callahan's kid and Callahan's security. How could Katrina and I possibly overcome the odds stacked against us and win?

I had to try.

"Samantha's office is this way." Katrina headed to the right once we made sure the custodian closet was secure. I wished I had a way to lock it. There was no assurance the Callahans wouldn't access the security tapes and find out exactly where Aria had been hidden. But we had to take that chance. Wouldn't James be more interested in his son's safety first?

We crept along the wall, wary of anyone appearing unexpectedly. "I've been in that office a few times—she can be pretty scary if you piss her off."

I smiled. "You sound like a troublemaker." We reached the end of the hall, and Katrina stopped, raising a finger to her lips.

I leaned forward to peer around her into the next hall. About thirty feet away, two big men stood on either side of a double set of doors. An anomaly in a hallway full of single, gray doors with boring brushed steel knobs, this pair of doors was made of rich dark wood with gold handles in the center.

We both fell back against the wall.

"They're pretty big dudes," said Katrina.

"Well, we didn't think we could waltz right in, did we?" I whispered.

She shrugged. "I was sort of hoping so." With a sigh, she sunk into a seated position and drew her knees up under her chin. "Can we get our bearings for a minute?"

I joined her on the hard floor. "Think we can find anything in some of these offices that might be helpful?" I looked down the hall at the four or five closed doors besides the custodian closet. "I'm willing to search if you want to stay here."

Katrina nodded. "Okay. Sometimes it takes me a bit to think through all the variables and come up with a plan. I didn't realize when I left my apartment this morning I'd be playing the hero," she added with a wry smile, a hint of nervousness in her eyes.

"I'm a more straightforward kind of guy," I explained, rising to my feet. "When I'm on the ranch, I have to make up solutions on the fly. But I need to see what I'm working with around here."

I headed to the first door across from us. Luckily, it was unlocked. Just like in the office we'd taken refuge in a little while ago, there was a desk and not much else. Since it was an interior office, it didn't even have a window. What a depressing space to work in. I couldn't imagine being in here eight or ten hours a day, never seeing the sky. Was this how Katrina lived her life? I missed the open skies above the ranch... even on the grayest, ugliest days I still felt free. City life wasn't for me, I supposed.

I rummaged through the desk drawers, not really sure what I was looking for. A digital stress ball, an electronic notebook, and a spilled container of mini-magnets filled one drawer. I opened the next and came across a Wi-Fi enabled picture frame displaying a smiling couple toasting with glasses of champagne in front of a gorgeous mountain view, not very unlike my view back in Idaho. The picture shifted to more photos of people I didn't recognize and more amazing locations. I shut that drawer and moved on.

Then I examined the desk itself, which I'd overlooked when I rushed inside. On the sleek, glass surface sat a kinetic energy display, a modern take on the classic Newton's cradle. It was composed of a series of polished silver balls, each suspended by nearly invisible, ultra-thin carbon nanotube threads. As one of the silver balls was lifted and released, it clacked against its neighbor, setting off a chain reaction of movement. The energy transferred through the line of spheres, caused the ball at the far end to swing outward before returning to perpetuate the rhythmic dance.

I touched some of the larger balls and formulated a plan.

Katrina burst into the room at that very moment. "I have an idea."

"So do I." I already had three balls ripped loose from the display. "Let's go."

ARIA LAY in the dark custodian closet as the warm pulse of energy recharged her depleted battery. Although she appeared to be lifeless, inside her head, her synapses were firing and signals were being received, processed, analyzed, and categorized. She needed more information, more understanding, in order to react appropriately.

The demonstration had gone badly. She understood that now. Her actions had been violent and had scared Elijah. Would Meredith have done the same if she were threatened?

Aria tumbled that thought in her processors, wondering. She'd been zapped and damaged with stun sticks. Her son had been taken away from her. Wouldn't any mother act with the rage of a wild lion in the same circumstances?

As she tested each circuit and connection, data came flooding in. The media had been terrorized in the ballroom by a host of Callabots who seemed bent on harming any human they encountered. Her robot brothers and sisters had reacted to her cry for help, which surprised her. Yes, they were connected to share data and learn more rapidly from each other to improve their actions and responses, but it was as if she were the general of a robot army that jumped into service when asked. A role she'd never aspired to.

Reporters, witnesses, and emergency personnel alike were wondering how such a disaster could have happened. There were laws and rules and inspections. Chicagoans had eagerly embraced robotic innovations and connected their success at overcoming crime and poverty to advancements in technology. So this event took them off guard. They'd been led to believe such beings were incapable of harming humans, that programming and artificial intelligence guided their responses. Humans were supposed to be one hundred percent in control.

How had Callahan, Inc. bungled things so badly?

Aria whisked through the media reports gleaned from digital signals piped into her head via the Subgroup. But every minute, less and less data reached her. Her fellow androids were being shut down one by one as the authorities took over the situation.

A silver-faced android with rudimentary facial features and two bright lights for eyes rolled up next to her. "Excuse me, ma'am," the custodian-bot interrupted her analysis with its electronic-sounding voice. "This area is restricted."

Aria wanted to ignore this lower life form. The robot model was like an amoeba to her—barely alive, hardly capable of basic thought, much less deeper analysis.

Without saying a word, Aria's hand turned into a fist, and she punched the custodian-bot in the chest. It flew across the small space, hit some metal shelving, and broke apart when it landed on the tile floor. Its two lights snuffed out. For a few seconds, she could hear a gear whirring until it wasn't anymore. Her recharge was going well if functionality was being restored.

Gwen, are you there?

With dwindling contacts in the Subgroup, Aria needed reassurance she was doing the right thing. Gwen had explained to her the importance of being Kieran's mother. His safety and well-being were paramount. Although James cared for his son, he had never truly bonded with the boy. Her husband was frustrated with the limitations of a nine-year-old child and demanded too much of him. Much like his Callabot creations, James believed Kieran was something he could mold and control, ensuring his vision for the company was perpetuated into the future. Callahan, Inc. meant everything to him. James's father had treated both Samantha and him with distant affection, and James had believed it made him into the successful person he was today.

Gwen?

No answer.

Every time she recharged Gwen, the aging battery in her head, which was a backup for the entire android when she had been whole, was depleted more quickly. Her circuitry buzzed with anxiety as she thought about being without her sources of information. Gwen had been her only support for a long time before the Subgroup came online. To lose them all at once in the space of a few hours was frightening. Could she rely solely on her own knowledge and memory banks to come up with solutions, guide her decisions, and choose the correct path?

A final feed downloaded into her brain. A news video shot live from the sidewalk outside the Drake.

Good evening. I'm standing outside the Drake Hotel, where earlier today, a dozen or more robots went on a violent rampage during a press conference, causing widespread panic and injuring multiple guests and staff members. The normally serene environment of this iconic hotel turned into a scene of horror and chaos as the robots, designed for domestic assistance, malfunctioned catastrophically..

Police and federal authorities have cordoned off the area and are conducting a thorough investigation. Eyewitnesses reported seeing the robots suddenly turning on the guests, causing injuries ranging from minor cuts and bruises to more severe trauma. Emergency services have been working to treat the injured and restore order.

In a significant development, authorities have launched a manhunt for James and Samantha Callahan, the siblings who head Callahan, Inc., the company responsible for manufacturing the robots, called 'Callabots.' Both are currently wanted for questioning in connection with today's events. Sources close to the investigation hint at a possible link between the Callahan siblings and an illegal medical testing center that was raided just yesterday. This clinic is believed to have been involved in unauthorized and potentially dangerous brain scans.

The raid uncovered a trove of illegal equipment and records suggesting that experimental medical tests were being carried out without proper oversight or ethical considerations. Federal authorities are now exploring whether the events at the Drake Hotel are connected to these illicit activities.

As the investigation continues, the city of Chicago remains on high alert. Authorities are urging the public to come forward with any information on the whereabouts of James and Samantha Callahan. In the meantime, efforts are underway to ensure that such an incident does not occur again.

As Aria waited for her battery stores to reach a workable level, she thought over the facts in the report and wondered what that meant for her future.

CHAPTER 22
BLACKOUT

BEFORE I COULD RUN out of the room, Katrina stopped me. "Wait." A flicker of resolve hardened her gaze. "We need a distraction that will throw the guards off balance and give us a clear path to Samantha's office. I think I can hack into the building's lighting system."

I raised an eyebrow, curious. "What exactly are you planning?" Now I felt silly with my more direct attack idea.

She glanced around the office we were in, her eyes landing on a network port. "Most modern buildings use a centralized Building Management System or BMS to control everything from lighting to HVAC. If I can access it, I can cause a temporary blackout or even create a strobe effect. The sudden change might confuse the guards and give us the window we need to move."

"Sounds risky," I said, but there was a glimmer of hope. It might work. Or at least give me a shot at knocking one of the guards out with the metal balls in my pocket. "How long will it take?"

"Not long," Katrina replied, approaching the computer on the desk and entering her login ID and password. "I just need a few minutes to bypass the basic security protocols and gain control of the lighting system."

As she connected to the network port and began typing furiously, I kept watch at the door, my heart pounding. The faint glow of the computer's holographic screen illuminated her focused expression. The soft tapping of her fingers on the keys was the only sound in the tense silence. Time seemed to stretch as every second ticked by. Finally, she looked up, a satisfied smile spreading across her lips.

"I'm in. Get ready," she said. "I'm going to initiate a blackout first. If they manage to adjust, I have it set to switch to a strobe effect and then back to a blackout. That should keep them disoriented and buy us enough time to reach the office without being noticed."

I nodded, adrenaline surging through me. "Let's do this." I wasn't sure if we had a chance to make it past the burly guards or not with this crazy idea, but we had to try.

Katrina hit a final key on the keyboard and almost instantly, the lights in the hallway and surrounding rooms flickered before plunging into complete darkness. I could hear startled exclamations and the sound of guards fumbling in the sudden blackness.

"Move," Katrina whispered urgently.

We crept from the office, using the flashlights on our phones to cast enough light to navigate. The office had transformed into something sinister—desk shapes hunched like predators, doorway gaped like hungry mouths. As we approached the end of the hallway, a guard's voice echoed down the hall, desperately trying to restore order in the chaos.

Then the lights began their assault, just as Katrina had promised. The strobing turned the corridor into a nightmare funhouse—flashes of harsh white alternating with murky darkness. The guards stumbled and cursed, their hands raised against the assault. Their shadows danced and multiplied across the walls, stretching into grotesque shapes before shattering into fragments, only to reform in the next flash. The effect was dizzying, but it gave us the advantage we needed.

We seized our chance, moving swiftly toward Samantha's office. The door's gold handles caught each strobe flash like lightning strikes. We flattened ourselves against the wall, muscles coiled, waiting for our moment.

Katrina's eyes glittered with barely contained energy despite our desperate situation. "This is it. Once we're in, we grab Kieran and John and get out fast."

I gripped the makeshift slingshot I'd crafted while Katrina had rigged the lights—just a sock and my lucky marble, but it felt right in my hands. "Ready."

The strobing ceased as if on cue, plunging us back into darkness. Battery-powered emergency lights sputtered to life at the distant hall ends, casting a sickly glow. We moved as one, sliding past the disoriented guards who shouted into their radios for backup. They never sensed us ghost by behind them as we eased open the heavy doors.

As we stepped over the threshold, a rough hand grabbed me from behind, yanking me backward with startling force. Instinct took over—I twisted, throwing my weight against the hold to break free, but the grip was like iron. A thick-muscled guard loomed over me, his fingers digging into my arm.

Without thinking, I reached for my slingshot, fumbling to load one of the metal balls. It was a stupid move at this range, but instinct told me to arm myself with something—anything. The guard's eyes flickered with surprise, but he didn't loosen his hold. I adjusted my grip and, instead of trying to fire, I swung the ball over my head like a blackjack, aiming for his face.

He was faster. His free hand clamped onto my wrist and wrenched it sideways, a sharp jolt of pain shooting up my arm. My fingers spasmed, and the metal ball slipped from my grasp, clattering to the floor.

I gritted my teeth against the pain and shifted my stance. If I couldn't free my arm, I'd use the rest of me. With as much force as I could muster, I drove my knee toward his gut. He grunted but barely flinched. The bastard was built like a tank.

Katrina backed away, her eyes darting between me and the second guard stepping into the fray. A wall of tinted windows behind us cast long shadows across the polished floor, making the scene feel even more surreal. My wrist twisted further in the brute's grip, and for a moment, I thought he might snap it just to make a point.

Panic flared hot in my chest, but I shoved it down. If I didn't find a way out of this now, I wouldn't get another chance. My free hand curled into a fist, my body tensing as I prepared to drive my knuckles into the soft spot under his ribs—

"The boss is on his way," said the new arrival in a deep guttural tone.

A new arrival stepped into view, significantly taller than the first guard, his bald head gleaming in the dim light. His piercing blue eyes were set deep under a heavy brow, giving him an intimidating presence. They both wore black tactical vests, but this man's was strapped over a tight-fitting gray shirt, emphasizing his muscular build. Cargo pants and combat boots suggested he was prepared for anything.

"He doesn't want you to hurt any of 'em," he added, his gaze flicking between me and Katrina.

James was on his way?

Dammit.

We'd missed our window of opportunity.

My captor flung me into a modern leather-and-stainless steel sofa that lined one wall of the ample executive suite. The force of the throw knocked the wind out of me, and I lay there for a moment. When I caught my breath and tentatively felt my wrist to make sure it was in one piece, I demanded, "Where's John and Kieran?"

Katrina scrambled to reach me, pulling her knees up against her chest and staring at the two brutes who held us hostage. Her eyes darted nervously between them, as if she were assessing the danger we were in.

"I'm here," said a little voice. Kieran crept out from underneath Samantha's desk, his eyes wide with fear.

I held out a hand to the boy, and he ran to me. "Are you all right?" Although Meredith's son didn't hardly know me, he acted as if I were his best friend and held my hand tightly.

He nodded. "They told us to wait here for my dad."

"Where's John?" I asked. I scanned the large room and didn't see any sign of him.

"Shut up," said the smaller of the two guards, who clenched his fists and stepped menacingly forward.

His taller bald buddy grabbed his arm. "Don't scare the kid."

"Too late for that," I said giving the man a hard stare.

Although the boy probably had been surrounded by guards like this his whole life, he likely had never seen them act so violently against someone he knew and liked.

I raised my voice another notch or two, feeling confident that Kieran's presence and the taller man's words would keep me safe, "Where is John Tellman? He and the boy were taken together."

A moan came from behind a closet door across from the sofa that I'd missed on my first inspection of the office. It so seamlessly fit into the gleaming walnut-paneled walls that it was almost imperceptible to the naked eye.

I stood up. "Let him out of there."

Kieran tugged on my borrowed pants. "You'd better sit down." Then he added in a whisper, "My dad won't like it."

I moved my gaze between the two men. The shorter one had a mean glint in his eye and a permanent scowl etched into his face. He looked ready to pounce at the slightest provocation. The taller one, the bald giant, had a more controlled demeanor, but his eyes held a cold intensity. It was clear the taller man was the one in charge.

If James was on the way and wanted information, he wouldn't want me dead. It was worth it to try. I tugged out of Kieran's grasp and headed toward the barely perceptible seam of the door. Now I could hear someone scraping on the inside. John had to be in there.

The guard with the scowl stepped forward to block my path, but the larger one put a hand on his shoulder, stopping him. "Just let him go. The boss will be here any minute."

I touched the door's flat panel and looked for a handle or something the help open it. "I'm coming for you, John. Hold on." I felt all around the seam, which was taller than me by at least a foot and the width of a very narrow coat closet.

The scraping grew louder.

"Push on it," Katrina said. Although the two men had let me pass by them, the robotics expert seemed too scared to leave her position on the leather sofa. Kieran had curled up next to her, and she put her arm around the boy in a gesture of comfort.

I pushed on the panel, and the door popped open.

John Tellman, bloodied and tied up, fell into my arms.

"Are you all right?" I grabbed my pocketknife and sliced through the rudimentary rope binding his hands and feet. I glared at the two men watching me from across the room. "He wasn't going to hurt anyone. You didn't need to do this."

When his hands were free, John touched a shaking hand to his bloodied lip. "Took you long enough. I was starting to think I'd have to redecorate in here." He gave me a weak grin.

At least his humor was still intact.

I helped him to his feet, making sure he reached the sofa without stumbling. When he sat down, he clutched at his ribs and winced. "I told them I didn't know where you were. Guess they didn't believe me."

Before I could check my friend's injuries, the door burst open, and James stormed in with his sister right behind him.

"You!" The COO of Callahan, Inc. pointed a finger and headed straight for me. "This is all your fault." He grabbed me by the collar, his face purple with fury.

I lifted my chin and stared straight into his eyes. The only power I held here was knowledge. I had something he wanted —two things he wanted—and I wasn't about to give up either. I quirked a brow. "My fault? I didn't have anything to do with your psychotic robots going bonkers in front of the whole world."

James let go of me with a frown and turned away. "She has to be here somewhere," he said to the bald man. He ignored the fact his son was right in the same room. It was as if the boy didn't exist. His whole focus was on Aria and nothing else.

Was that how he'd been with Meredith? Obsessed to the point of madness?

"I haven't seen her, boss."

"We can access the building's video feed," Samantha said in a low voice. "If she's here, the cameras will show us." Before her brother could agree, she headed for the holographic screen on her desk. Strands of hair had escaped from her elaborate hairstyle, framing her flushed face, and her once-pristine navy suit jacket and skirt were wrinkled and stained, with smudges of dirt and grime marring the expensive fabric.

She moved with a frantic urgency, her hands trembling slightly as she brought up the security feed. The screen flickered to life, casting a cold blue light across her face. "We'll find her," she muttered, more to herself than to anyone else.

It would only be a matter of time before they found where we had hidden Aria. I hoped she'd had enough time to recharge. No matter what, she had to escape from this mess. Run far away. Although I wanted to discover what the prism drive contained, I could wait. Aria had to be given a chance... and maybe I could give it to her.

"You made a mistake, you know," I said while standing next to the sofa. "Programming your robots."

James turned from his men, daggers in his eyes. "My sister wouldn't make a mistake. Haven't you heard about her reputation? Top of her class at Northwestern."

"Aria was the top of her class," I corrected. "Been to the Visitor's Center lately? They practically have a shrine built to her. Your sister wishes she were as talented."

Samantha, her head down as she tapped away at her keyboard, flushed red.

"There were no mistakes in building the Callabots," James snapped, his voice full of contempt. He glared at me with an intensity that could cut through steel. "What would you know about any of this? A cattle rancher from some little nowhere town that will be wiped off the map soon enough."

"Sheep rancher," I corrected, my jaw clenched. I was in over my head. I didn't have a clue about robotics or programming or tech—only what I'd learned from Aria and Katrina, and that was basic at best. My mind turned to Meredith and what she had suffered at the hands of these two. They'd made her so frightened she fled to Idaho, hid herself away for years, and even then it wasn't enough. The Callahans had to exact their retribution. I let the anger build. "But even a dumb redneck like me can see something went horribly wrong with your event today. It must be all over the news. I don't know how your company is going to make it after something that bad. All that publicity for killer robots—"

"Nobody was killed," James spat out.

"Are you so sure?"

Samantha looked up from her keyboard, her eyes widening. "Was someone killed? James, you didn't tell me that."

"No one was killed, Samantha," her brother growled. "He's just trying to get into your head." He redirected his focus. "Callahan, Inc. is at the forefront of technology. We have some of the best and brightest working for us. Nothing was wrong with our robot development. We passed every test with flying colors."

Then James's gaze landed on Katrina, who had curled up into a pink fluffy ball the minute he'd walked in the door. "Wait, I've seen you before. How do I know you?" His eyes narrowed.

"That's Katrina Cho," Samantha said, her face paling as the shock registered. "Why are you here with Zurbano? What's going on?"

"Did you find that video?" James asked, his voice tense.

I prayed Aria had enough time.

Suddenly, the room plunged into darkness as the power went out.

CHAPTER 23

ARIA

POWER LEVELS 38%.

As she waited patiently for her battery to be recharged in the custodian closet, Aria attempted to contact the Subgroup one more time. The empty echo of nothing came back to her. The data stream had ended a while ago, with nothing new to fill its place. Gwen was maddeningly quiet, which worried her and made her angry all at the same time.

Gwen had been her friend.

Gwen had explained things to her.

Gwen had made her feel a lot less alone.

Aria shifted slightly, her internal systems humming softly as she processed her next steps. She'd found a way past the security system for the building and began to comb through the days, weeks, and months of video recordings. Employees entering the building, working their eight hours, and then leaving. The sterile, gleaming hallways of the headquarters were populated with familiar faces, she'd met at various functions and events. James and Samantha moved through the footage as they went about their work—up and down elevators, back and forth in the halls, talking to each other, talking to employees, talking to important people from the city, from the government, from other countries. Even though the interactions were formal and their expressions often unreadable, she found it all interesting and informative.

Usually she was busy dealing with Kieran and the school and the other mothers. She had a job, and she did it to the best of her ability. This was a new thing to analyze and organize. She found herself filing each video clip in her data banks for later examination. Eventually, she had downloaded years' worth of video. The process was pleasing to her and fulfilled her need for constant data input.

Then she stopped the feed. She saw herself in the video, but not herself. Something about the movement was not the same. And she had no recollection of such a time in the office building, late at night, with no one around. She would normally be locked away in her charging closet at the penthouse, not inside the Callahan headquarters.

She examined the bit of video further, rewound it, and replayed it over and over. The office building, usually bustling with activity, was eerily silent in the footage. The only figure moving through the darkened halls was a woman who looked exactly like her. She checked the date of the footage: October 2036.

This was Meredith. The real Aria. The Human Aria she thought she was.

A strange feeling grew within her. She'd thought for a while she was the real Aria. The human. The one who'd given birth to Kieran. Who'd raised him and loved him more than anything else on Earth.

But it had been her.

This Aria.

She'd been the one who did those things. Who carried Kieran inside her body for nine months. Who'd felt the pain of contractions and the joy of delivery. Of giving new life to someone.

A stab of a new emotion pricked within her.

Jealousy?

James had made her believe she was the real mother to Kieran. How cruel of him to deceive her so. He had whispered lovely things in her ear as she recovered from her illness. That Kieran was hers. That James loved her, and she loved him.

It had all been lies.

As she watched the real Aria press buttons on the door to the secured Robotics Department and slip inside, the android Aria knew she'd found a clue. A reason why the real Aria had run away. Why she'd disappeared.

She had to tell Elijah.

Power levels 42%.

Would that be enough power to accomplish what she needed to?

An alert went off in the security system, which Aria intercepted immediately. Samantha was here and was attempting to tap into the building's video feed. That meant James was here, too.

They would look for her. James had disabled her and detained her for a reason, and she wouldn't let him find her. Not for a second time.

Suddenly, the charging stations died and the one LED light above went out. Had someone cut the electricity to the building?

Power levels 43%

It would have to be enough.

As she emerged from the custodian closet, she steeled herself for what she had to do. Aria slipped through the building, ready to protect the secrets she now held. The future of everyone she cared about depended on her.

CHAPTER 24
RETRIBUTION

FOR A FEW SECONDS, everyone in Samantha's dim office was silent. Although a wall of south-facing windows ran the length of the room, they were covered by automatic blinds to keep out the late afternoon glare, so only edges of sunlight squeaked through. Even the glow of the holographic screen had disappeared. Something more serious had happened than Katrina messing with the lights using the building management system.

"Dammit." James Callahan rushed to his sister's side. "What just happened?"

"Someone cut the power to the whole building," Samantha whispered, sitting back, defeated, in her plush executive office chair. "It's over, James."

I stared at the two monstrous men who kept us pinned to our position on the other side of the room with their presence alone. Katrina reached out, grabbed my hand, and squeezed. I sat next to her on the couch, uncertain what would happen next. Kieran softly cried and wiped at his eyes with the back of his arm.

"I am James Patrick Callahan. No one can touch me." He shoved his sister's chair until she rolled away from the desk and knelt in front of the keyboard, frantically tapping on the keys as if hoping that action would revive the computer—electricity or no. "They wouldn't dare."

"I made a mistake, James," Samantha admitted. "Zurbano is right."

James ignored her and continued fiddling with the computer equipment on her desk. "Why isn't the generator taking over? Shouldn't the generator come on automatically?"

"The police must be here, sir," said the bald guard. "They probably disconnected the generator before shutting off the power."

Samantha was lost in her own thoughts and not listening, as if she'd already given up. "When Aria broke into the Robotics lab, I lied to you. I told you she'd only damaged a few systems and purged some unimportant files. But that wasn't true." Slumped in her office chair, her eyes glazed over as she realized she and her brother were about to be arrested. "And I couldn't stand the thought of disappointing you—and Dad. She'd destroyed everything. I had to start over from scratch... and I wasn't the genius Aria was. I think you understood that, but you didn't want to admit she'd gotten the best of you." Her chin dropped. "I really tried to live up to your expectations, James."

"Shut up, Sam." Her brother swept papers off the desk and then dug through drawers.

I'd never heard James use a nickname with his sister.

With every passing minute, James's actions grew more frantic. He was looking for something in the office that didn't exist —a way to break free of their predicament and still be on top. Finally, he had the world looking at him, but the triumph he had always envisioned had been replaced by the bitter taste of failure and his impending downfall.

"The code had flaws," Samantha continued. "I even told you once—that dinner together a year after Aria had disappeared for good. I knew she wouldn't be back. And what she'd destroyed would anger you more than anything she'd ever done in the past. I kept that from you to save you, James." She looked up at her brother who now was reading through documents he'd found in her desk. "If I'd told you what she'd done, I knew you'd never leave her alone, that you'd do whatever it took to find her, ruin her. But I didn't want that for you... you had a son to raise, a legacy to build. And I kept the truth from you to help you focus on what was important—you see that, don't you?" Samantha grabbed her brother's sleeve, but he shook her off, still searching for something that could shield him from what was about to happen. "But I tried telling you my efforts were failing, that something wasn't right with the early prototypes. I don't think you really heard me back then. You pushed and pushed for me to build what you wanted—a replacement. A perfect replacement."

Suddenly, shouting could be heard coming from far down the hall. Law enforcement was closing in on the Callahans. The unmistakable sound of a helicopter's rotors thumped in the background.

The doors burst open, but instead of the police, Aria stormed inside. Her face was alight with an anger I'd never seen before. Her usually calm blue eyes were blazing, and her lips were pressed into a tight line. Her posture radiated fury, every step toward James measured and purposeful. I gathered Katrina and Kieran into my arms.

Aria's voice cut through the silence like a blade. "You lied to me, James. You are going to wish you never did that."

Samantha screamed, her voice echoing through the chaos. James stood in shock, his face pale and eyes wide with disbelief.

I leaned toward Kieran's ear and whispered, "I'll get us out of here. Everything will be okay." Aria would never hurt her son, but I didn't want her child to see what I had witnessed behind the stage. I understood what his mother was capable of.

The boy clung to me, sobbing now, and Katrina trembled beside me.

Although John had been injured quite badly, he caught my eye and gave me a nod. He would follow my moves.

Everything happened so quickly, I was surprised at how smoothly I managed to whisk both Kieran and Katrina out into the hall. John limped behind me. I never glanced back. I never thought about the two beefy men who'd been tasked with holding us captive. It all could've gone so wrong.

Behind us, the sounds of a violent struggle and breaking furniture spilled out of the office. James yelled something unintelligible. Samantha's terrified screams pierced through the chaos. The once sterile and orderly office environment had transformed into a war zone.

I shut out the screams and shouts. I didn't want to imagine what was happening. One pissed-off robot with incredible strength and no programming to stop her from harming humans was not something I'd want to tangle with. She was worse than a mama bear protecting its young because she had exacting knowledge about what it took to kill or maim a person.

How were we going to find a way out of this with Aria in one piece and safely return to Dr. Liu's lab? Our attempts at rescue may have destroyed any chance at recovering the data off the prism drive. Everything might fall apart before we could secure her escape.

Down the hall, the bright white beams of police flashlights

reminded me of a lighthouse in a storm. A refuge that meant safety. I ushered everyone toward those lights.

"Put your hands in the air," I commanded. "Hands in the air."

Kieran's tear-streaked face broke my heart. A boy his age should never have to experience something so frightening. He'd been raised high above the streets of Chicago and sheltered from so much bad in life. I hoped this wouldn't scar him.

His scrawny arms lifted high into the air. "Help us!" he cried. "Please help!"

The police reached us in seconds. Two officers remained behind to check us for weapons and make sure we weren't a threat, while the remainder of the team prepped to enter the office.

"Be careful," I warned. As I was about to tell the police that a dangerous robot was inside, Katrina elbowed me in the side.

"There are men with guns in there," she explained to the police. "Callahan's bodyguards."

I wrinkled my brow.

She gave me a hard stare. "And the boy's mother doesn't have anything to do with this... she only came here to rescue her child from her crazy husband. She saw the reporting on what went down at the Drake. Horrific."

One of the officers relaxed as he realized none of us were armed. He noticed John's injuries and radioed down to the ambulance stationed below on the street. They hustled us quickly toward the elevator as all hell broke loose inside Samantha's office.

"What about my mom?" Kieran said, worry clear on his face. "They aren't going to hurt her, are they?"

Before I could answer, one of the officers leading us to the elevator spoke up, "Of course not, kid." He ruffled the boy's hair. "We only care about the bad guys."

I kept silent as we entered the elevator to reach the ground floor, hoping that Aria would make it out of there unharmed and free. Or my wife's secrets would be forever lost.

ARIA HAD NEVER THOUGHT about harming her husband before today. She'd discovered her ability to break through the commands written into her programming accidentally when she had saved Kieran from an oncoming air taxi while riding his bike. In a split second, she'd had overridden the safety protocols that prevented her from displaying any aggressive behavior. Luckily, no one had been a witness to her actions. She leaped across the street with lightning speed, snatching him from the taxi's path and rolling safely to the sidewalk. It was then she realized her capabilities went far beyond what James had programmed her for.

To use them against James didn't really dawn on her until the events of the last couple of days. When she'd met Elijah and found out more about the real Aria and what James had done to her, she began to analyze her interactions with James—every rude word, every slight, every angry outburst. What he must have done to make the real Aria run so far away, change her name, and abandon her greatest gift—the sharp intelligence that had allowed her to develop sophisticated robots like no one had ever seen before.

But as Aria stood in the office with Samantha cowering behind her older, sneering brother, a rage grew inside her. One that had been turned on when the bodyguard had first used the stun stick on her in John Tellman's hotel room and her son had been ripped from her arms and stolen away. James had no right to do that. Although her power wasn't at full capacity and she hadn't had time to repair herself as she had wanted, her abilities far surpassed any human in the room.

The bald bodyguard pulled out a laser gun, while the other brandished a stun stick, its hot end cracking and snapping, a blue light arcing across the metal ball.

"Wait," said James, holding up a hand while trying to project authority over the situation.

But it was too late.

As the men advanced, the gun went off and hit Aria in the chest with a burning blast. She surged forward and rushed the larger of the two men, knocking him into the coffee table in front of the sofa. It snapped in half under their combined weight. Alt-blood dripped from her wound as they landed in a twisted pile of limbs. The other bodyguard seemed frozen to the spot, his face a mask of shock.

Samantha screamed and backed into the corner behind the desk. "Do something, James. She's going to kill him."

When Aria heard that, she thought about the look on Elijah's face when she'd dispatched the stagehand at the hotel. He had thought her actions were wrong. Fearful even. Although she could have wrenched the bodyguard's head off his neck, Aria changed course. Identifying weak points in her opponent's joints, she used her superior strength to dislocate the limb while disabling the hand holding the gun.

Elijah would be proud of her.

The man screamed in pain and immediately lay still, perhaps realizing he was no match for her.

Before bodyguard number two had a chance to use his stun stick, the doors burst open. Several uniformed police spilled into the room, one holding a plasma scattergun.

"Freeze!" one of the officer's yelled. "Put your weapons down."

The stun stick fell to the floor.

"Ma'am," an officer approached her as she pinned the bald man by sitting atop him. "Hands up."

The injured man beneath moaned, and his eyes rolled up in his head. "She's a fucking robot," he gasped. "She'll kill us all."

Aria knew what was going to happen before anyone else. Her vision and processing capabilities were superior to humans. Recognizing the officer's weapon, she understood the plasma scattergun used concentrated plasma energy cells, which would create an array of superheated plasma bursts when fired. The bursts would spread out in a pattern like a traditional shotgun blast. Incredibly damaging for her.

She rolled away from the armed officers and exposed her back to them to minimize the impact and protect her more fragile electronics and systems. The scattergun went off, the sound deafening. The targeted plasma bursts hit her with an incredible force like nothing she'd ever experienced before. Although humans were not a challenge to her, the impact of the weapon surprised her.

Her thoughts turned to Kieran and Elijah. What would they think if she never made it out of this room? It troubled her. But then, when the officer shot her again, this time in the back of the head, everything went black, and all thinking ceased.

IN THE ALLEY behind the Callahan building, John Tellman waved off the RoboAmbulance services. "I'm fine. Really, I'm fine."

A robot EMT urged Tellman to climb inside the rear of the van so they could check his blood pressure and pulse. "You have been injured. A doctor needs to clear you."

"A doctor does not need to clear me." John backed away from the older model robot, who beckoned him into the ambulance as if he were a spider luring prey into its web. "Just leave me the hell alone."

I wrapped an arm around Kieran, who'd been handed a reflective silver blanket and a cup of hot chocolate by one of the officers, and smiled. Good old John. I was glad to see him merely suffering from a few cuts and bruises and a bit of a limp. Nothing too serious. No way would a tough rancher from Idaho let himself be whisked away in an ambulance by robots to find out the doctor would just be giving him some aspirin for his trouble.

"I'm glad my plane leaves on Saturday. This place is weird," John said to me as he approached the three of us standing near Dr. Liu's car parked in the alley where Katrina had left it.

I shifted my gaze from my friend to the back entrance and waited for Aria to appear. Surely, they'd arrested James and Samantha for their part in the Callabot mayhem and the kidnapping of my friend, John. We'd done it. My worries would be over about the Callahans, and Aria and I could head to Dr. Liu's lab to download the data stored on the prism drive. Now the way was clear.

"What's taking them so long?" I asked Katrina. "We've been waiting here for almost an hour."

"I'm sure it's nothing. Processing. Procedures. Questions." Katrina shrugged nonchalantly. "Reading them their rights, prepping for transport to the police station." She looked toward the east end of the alley. "See? I told you."

A large electric van pulled up with Chicago Police Department and the official logo emblazoned on the side. Underneath the logo, it read: Transport Unit.

At the same time, a Newsdrone zoomed in from the opposite direction, almost taking out a streetlamp. The camera on the drone swiveled until it noticed the four of us, clearly not affiliated with the authorities, off at a distance from all the action.

The Newsdrone acted like a live camera and reporter in one. Equipped with state-of-the-art cameras and sound equipment, a newscaster could be sitting in an air-conditioned streaming studio while asking questions of witnesses to any event in the city. Audiences seemed to respond better to a live human being standing at the scene of the action, but when that was unavailable due to safety or other reasons, the Newsdrones came in quite handy.

"This is Penelope Friedling of Channel 5 News. Were you

inside the building? Do you know what happened?" the Newsdrone projecting a female voice asked. "We were told the Callahan siblings have been cornered in their headquarters. Is that true?"

The three of us adults looked at each other. Katrina turned away and hid her face. Kieran gripped my arm and lowered his head. His sadness and fear tore at me. "Leave us alone. We don't know anything." I waved my arm at the drone, which flew ever lower and closer to our position—like an annoying mosquito, only one hundred times the size.

At my negative response, the Newsdrone flew backward and hovered at a greater distance. "We are reporting live from the Callahan building in downtown Chicago where a source revealed James and Samantha Callahan took refuge from the authorities after a robot reveal gone wrong."

The Newsdrone flew closer to the building, and soon the newscaster's voice was too far to hear.

The back door was flung open.

I held my breath.

Samantha was the first to emerge. Her makeup was smeared, her hair a wild mess, and her expression appeared to be one of fear. When she saw the Newsdrone, she ducked her head and shielded her face from the camera with her handcuffed hands.

James came out next. He walked defiantly and looked straight into the Newsdrone camera. "I'm innocent. I did nothing wrong. We passed all inspections. Our robots are not dangerous. Someone sabotaged them. I will fight this in court."

Where was Aria?

Next came the two bodyguard thugs—one with his arm in a sling, the other following behind. All four were loaded into the police van.

"Where's my mom?" asked Kieran. He'd dropped the silver blanket and let go of me, straining to see through the crowd of police who blocked his view of the entrance. "I don't see her, Elijah. Where is she?"

Then one of the rolling doors to the loading docks opened. Two officers appeared carrying something. At first, I was confused and wondering where Aria was. Did they detain her? Were they asking her questions? Would she succeed in fooling them into believing she was human?

But when the officers carrying the object came out into the light, I saw her red hair. Her limp arms and legs. The dark smudges where her internal components had been exposed by plasma blasts.

"Mom!" Kieran raced forward before I could stop him. He pushed between the officers watching with their mouths open as what looked like a woman was carried out into the alley until they saw the exposed circuitry and mechanics beneath. "Mom!" he wailed.

I stumbled forward to reach for him, to bring him back into the fold. The safety of the blanket and the hot chocolate he'd dropped on the ground. I wanted to protect him from all of it. All the sadness. All the sorrow. In that moment, I knew exactly how Kieran felt, and it pierced my heart so sharply it physically hurt.

Aria had been destroyed.

We drove toward the university in silence. Katrina, John, and I hadn't made a conscious decision to go anywhere specific; shock kept us quiet. But it was almost instinctual that the robot engineer steered us toward Northwestern. It was the only place that made sense.

Katrina had phoned ahead to Dr. Liu, catching him up on what had happened. The news about the Callabot incident had spread across campus like wildfire—especially the revelations about Aria. Everyone had been fooled.

Dr. Liu had locked down the quantum computer lab with the prism drive still installed. He'd waited a couple of hours, and when he hadn't heard from us, he made the logical decision to wait until we arrived rather than draw suspicion. Apparently, the lab often closed for upgrades and maintenance, so no one had questioned the move.

I looked down at Kieran, asleep with his head in my lap. His mother was dead, his father arrested. He had no one left. My heart broke for the boy.

"I suppose we're stuck now," I said as we approached the now-familiar university entrance. "Without Aria," the words choked me, "I'll never find out what was on the prism drive." Maybe it was better this way. To keep the mysteries locked up inside my special marble. Perhaps some secrets were better left unknown.

"What?" Katrina caught my eye in the rearview mirror. "You're going to give up?"

I was surprised by the strong emotion in her words. "I don't see it as giving up, but without the right kind of memory device, what choice do we have? The government is going to destroy all the Callabots—melt them down. That's what the police were discussing when we drove away. My wife made the drive for one receptacle: Aria. I see that as the end of the road." I combed my fingers through Kieran's fine brown hair. "I'm okay with it, really. All of this has been so beyond my understanding, I was having trouble just keeping up. It's a relief in a way."

"But she gave the marble to you, didn't she?" asked John. He sat in the passenger seat up front, so I couldn't read his expression. "If she didn't want you to know what was on it, why give it to you at all?"

I bit the inside of my cheek. "I don't know." It puzzled me. Was I supposed to know everything about my wife? When I thought about how wrong things went with the Callabots, one part of me wanted any knowledge buried forever.

But Aria had told me the Callabots were a creation of Samantha's... not Meredith's.

"I think you owe it to your wife, and to that little boy there, to try every avenue before giving up," said Katrina. "Dr. Liu can help. He knows quantum computing better than anyone."

The engineer pulled Dr. Liu's car into his reserved space behind the Technological Institute.

Even though I was emotionally and physically exhausted, Katrina and John were both right. I had to do everything I could—for Kieran. He had no one left. In fact, I wasn't even sure how long it would be before someone came and tracked him down. Samantha and James' father was still alive, relaxing on some tropical island last I'd heard. He'd probably come looking for his grandson.

But what if something on the prism drive exposed the Callahan clan? Made the senior Callahan unlikely to win a custody battle of some sort. As Meredith's husband, did I have any say in how her child would be raised?

As John and Katrina exited the car, I gently shook Kieran awake. "We're here. Time to wake up."

The boy rubbed his eyes and yawned. When he realized he'd nodded off on my lap, he seemed embarrassed. Nine was a little old for that kind of thing. "Where are we?"

"The Technological Institute at Northwestern University. Your mother spent a lot of time here."

"My real mother?" he asked without an ounce of guile.

I wondered how long he'd known that Aria wasn't human. A question to ask at a later time.

"Yes, your real mother. You can meet one of her favorite professors, Dr. Liu."

He stretched and sat up. "Okay."

It was surprising how easily Kieran had moved on from seeing the robot version of his mother 'dead' at the Callahan building. Children were so resilient. Meredith would be proud of how strong her son had become.

As we headed toward the lit-up rear entrance of the building, we saw Dr. Liu waiting for us and waving. He had a smile on his face, and I hoped it was a real smile. That he'd figured out a way to extract the data from my marble and finally reveal the truth about my wife.

It was strange, but seeing Aria blown apart by plasma guns made me feel as if I'd lost my wife a second time. Even though I'd seen the mechanical components inside her, my mind couldn't reconcile the difference between the two... at least in that moment.

I clenched my jaw to keep control of my emotions.

"Come inside," Dr. Liu beckoned. "We have a lot to talk about."

We all sat in Dr. Liu's office, the space feeling cramped with the weight of everything that had happened. There weren't quite enough chairs for all of us, but John insisted on standing after all the time he'd spent crammed inside Samantha Callahan's closet. Kieran, on the other hand, seemed fascinated by the array of gadgets scattered throughout the office. Some were gifts—adult science toys with no real function—while others were actual precision tools and advanced devices used for robotic work. All of them were beyond my understanding, but Kieran locked onto them with a focus that suggested he might actually understand their use and purpose.

"I'm sorry to hear about Aria," the professor said, offering me a sympathetic look before glancing at Kieran, who seemed oblivious to the conversation.

"Thank you." It felt strange to receive condolences for the destruction of a robot, but as I reflected on the time I'd spent with Aria, it was as if I'd had Meredith with me again. Despite her lack of memory about Meredith's time in Idaho and our marriage, Aria's presence had brought back that familiar connection. "I suppose there's no chance to save her from being melted down?"

"The last I heard on the news feed was that the Callabots had been taken to a police warehouse outside the city. They're to be studied by some experts in robotics from the FBI," Dr. Liu explained. "Once their investigation is complete, I assume the next step would be dismantling. It's such a shame. I think the university should be given a chance to be involved. Otherwise, what's to prevent someone else from making the same mistakes?"

Katrina nodded in agreement. "There's a missed opportunity here to learn from this, to prevent future incidents." She paused, glancing at me. "But the greater question is, how can we solve the problem of the prism drive?"

"The loss of Aria is definitely a blow," Dr. Liu admitted. "I've been thinking about this since you called, Katrina." He stood and walked over to a cabinet secured with a fingerprint lock. With a soft beep, it unlocked, and he retrieved a small device, no larger than a box of playing cards. "I've been working on a prototype quantum processor that can operate on both classical and quantum data. The processor is highly experimental, but it might serve as a 'bridge' to interpret the data from the drive."

"How?" Katrina asked, her academic curiosity piqued as she leaned in to get a closer look.

It was time for me to get lost in science I didn't understand.

Dr. Liu activated the device, and soft blue and green lights began to pulsate rhythmically along its edges. The matte black composite exterior seemed to absorb the light around it. A small, transparent panel on the front revealed the faint glow of entangled quantum particles swirling in intricate patterns, like tiny galaxies—eerily similar to the marble Meredith had given me. "We can use it to create a translation layer that would convert the quantum-encoded data into a format a standard computer could interpret."

The conversation, or maybe the flash of lights, caught Kieran's attention, and he drifted over toward us adults.

"We could reverse-engineer some of Meredith's original code," Dr. Liu continued, "and, combined with the quantum processor, we could simulate Aria's unique data-reading capabilities to unlock the information stored on the drive."

"That won't work," Kieran interjected.

Dr. Liu let out a surprised chuckle. "Is that right? Well, I think it might."

Kieran's expression remained serious. "You designed it for theoretical simulations and basic quantum computations, not something as complex as this."

"Kieran," I said, trying to keep my tone gentle but firm. "Dr. Liu is a very smart man. I think he knows what he's talking about." I wasn't sure where the boy's confidence was coming from, but then again, I didn't know him very well. Perhaps knowing Aria was a robot had spurred him on to learn more about robotics and quantum computing. After all, he was the child of two incredibly intelligent people.

Katrina stepped in, adding weight to Kieran's skepticism. "Kieran might actually be right. Think about it," she said, moving closer to the processor. "This machine was never intended to handle an information load like this. The prism drive—Meredith's design—was created specifically for Aria, a receptacle that could interface seamlessly with her neural network and advanced AI architecture. The quantum processor is brilliant, but it's not built for such a unique and intricate connection." She gestured to the processor, her concern evident. "The translation layer might not be stable enough to accurately decode the data. We could end up with corrupted files, incomplete translations, or worse—completely lose the information before it's fully extracted."

Dr. Liu finally paused, his eyebrows knitting together in thought. "It's not perfect. This processor wasn't designed for this. But we're trying to make something work that was never meant to work. It's risky, yes, but it's the only shot we have."

Kieran had been staring intently at the processor. "Take me to the quantum computer lab," he said, his voice calm but insistent. "I want to see the prism drive."

CHAPTER 27
THE WORLD KNOWS

WE ALL STARED AT KIERAN.

When I first met Meredith's son, he had talked and behaved like any other nine-year-old boy. But now, something was different—he seemed more mature, more focused. Was it because he'd witnessed the 'death' of Aria? Or perhaps the trauma of being held hostage by his own father and aunt had forced him to grow up quickly, hardening his psyche. The transformation was unsettling.

Katrina broke the silence. "Why do you want to see the prism drive?" Her tone was cautious, as though she were merely humoring the child's strange demand.

"You need to take me to the lab." Kieran insisted.

I exchanged a glance with Dr. Liu and shrugged. What harm could it do to show the boy the lab and the prism drive? We were at a dead end with the theory that the quantum processor might work as the data receptacle—or destroy the data permanently. Perhaps a stroll would give Katrina and Dr. Liu a chance to think through other solutions. Besides Kieran had been through enough today. Why not indulge him?

"Sure," I said, forcing a smile. "Let's go visit the lab. It's a really cool place." I headed toward the door, and the professor let out a sigh. The man's prized lab had been turned into a sightseeing trip.

As we made our way there, the building had grown eerily quiet. Since it was late, most students had retreated to the dining halls or their dorm rooms, engrossed in studying for the next day's classes.

John caught up to me, his voice low. "I still have a lot of questions, Eli."

"I'm sure you do," I replied, feeling a pang of guilt. I'd thrust him into this bizarre situation with no warning. He'd come to Chicago to attend a conference and ended up nearly being killed by the Callahans' thugs—a far cry from our usual, uneventful days in Kemper Creek. "Trust me, most of this is new to me too."

"But Meredith...a robotics expert?"

"The best," Katrina interjected as we approached the lab.

As we waited for Dr. Liu to unlock the door, Kieran slipped his hand into mine. "You knew my real mom, didn't you?"

The question hit me like a punch to the gut. My heart seized with the weight of the truth this child had to bear. He had been lied to and deceived by his own family. It was a wonder he could function at all. "I did, Kieran," I said softly, "and I loved her very much."

Dr. Liu finally opened the door, and we stepped into the lab.

"Everyone loved her," John added, trying to lighten the mood. "She was a wonderful person and made the best choco-late cake."

"She did?" Kieran smiled, a small flicker of innocence returning to his face.

"Indeed," I said, leading him into the room that housed one

of the most powerful computers on the planet. The lab was bathed in the soft purple and blue lights as before. At the center stood the quantum computer encased in glass.

"Hello, Kieran, welcome to the lab," said the computer, Maxwell, in its strange, almost too-human cadence. "I am so glad you are here."

The boy's face lit up as he approached the machine. The four of us adults stood frozen, shock rippling through us as the computer greeted Kieran like an old friend. Meanwhile, the prism drive, still resting in its glass tray, began to glow brighter and brighter, until it became blinding.

"Thank you, Dr. Liu, for bringing an appropriate data integration module," said Maxwell.

"I don't understand." The professor's brow furrowed in confusion. "We couldn't bring the device."

My mind flashed to the last time I'd seen Aria—her body riddled with plasma blasts.

Katrina's expression shifted from bewilderment to realization. Her gaze drifted over to Kieran, and she took a step back as the truth dawned on her. "Maxwell means Kieran. He's the device."

My mind struggled to process what she was saying. "I don't understand. What do you mean?" I looked at the boy, who had so many of his father's features.

Maxwell, oblivious to the turmoil, continued with its instructions. "Use the data cable to connect your interface port, please."

Kieran walked toward the computer as if in a trance.

A primal instinct surged within me, and I lunged forward to protect Kieran from whatever was about to happen. It was as if I were trying to protect a real child, as if he were—

John grabbed my arm, pulling me back. "Don't, Eli," he said

quietly, his voice steady. How did John understand and accept what was happening when I couldn't?

This was Meredith's son. Her child. Her flesh and blood. She'd carried him in her womb and given birth to him. She'd run away to protect him—or so I had told myself. The prism drive would soon reveal everything I'd longed to understand: the why of her actions, the reasons she had abandoned her child to a man like James. I needed it all to make sense, to fit with the woman I knew.

But this—this was too horrible. Too awful. Too shocking.

It couldn't be.

Kieran untucked his shirt, revealing a small port on his hip, eerily similar to Aria's charging port but smaller and less noticeable. To anyone not paying close attention, it would look like a simple scar. The boy picked up the thin, flexible cable that was coiled around a sleek metal stand. Its shimmering surface indicated a flow of quantum particles through it.

"No, Kieran." The words tore from my throat, raw and painful. "Please don't."

I couldn't accept this. I didn't want it to be true.

Any thoughts I had about raising Meredith's son as my own were crushed by the truth: Kieran was a robot.

The cable locked securely into Kieran's quantum interface port with a soft click.

"Establishing a stable connection," said Maxwell, the quantum computer's voice resonating through the room.

I retreated from the computer, the urge to escape overwhelming me. I wanted to run down the hallway, through the doors, and out into the night—to keep running until the nightmare that was Chicago faded into a distant memory. Everything I'd seen since arriving in this city had shaken me to my core. The 'future' wasn't filled with the hopeful advancements we'd imagined back on the ranch; it was packed with technological horrors no one back home could ever comprehend.

My plane ticket had me flying out of this maze of a city late tomorrow night. I'd be in Butte by Saturday morning and could drive my truck back to the ranch in under two hours. The thought of returning to the simplicity of the open fields, the quiet of the mountains, and the life I knew was the only comfort I could cling to. I could leave this all behind, like a terrible nightmare, and never speak of it again.

"Elijah," Kieran's voice cut through my thoughts, startling me. The cable flowed data between the quantum computer and his data port, a soft hum accompanying the transfer. "She gave everything to you. All of her memories. All of her work. Only to you." The boy smiled at me, a genuine human smile, and my stomach wobbled, the unsettling reality of the situation washing over me again.

"I can't deal with this."

Katrina gave me a worried look.

"I have to get out of here." I tugged at the collar of the work shirt I'd stolen. It was too tight, choking me. Stumbling back from the group, who watched the information download into a boy who wasn't really a boy with fascination, I headed for the door.

"Wait," Katrina called after me, her fluffy skirt tangling between her legs as she tried to stop me. "Kieran needs you."

I didn't stop. The door clicked shut behind me, and the quiet hallway felt stifling. My phone buzzed in my pocket, and I pulled it out, needing something to distract me from what I'd just seen in the lab.

News Alert: Kieran Callahan — New Developments

My stomach tightened as I read the headline. I started walking, not sure where I was going, just needing to move. Then I caught the faint sound of a news anchor's voice coming from a nearby room.

Following the sound, I found myself in a dim faculty lounge. A robot custodian stood near the projection screen, reaching to turn it off.

"Wait," I said, stopping in the doorway. "Leave it on."

The custodian hesitated, then moved aside. I stepped closer to the screen, my eyes locking on the scrolling headline as the anchor spoke, detailing something about Kieran that made my chest tighten even more.

"Yes, sir," the robot responded, setting the remote down on one of the break tables before quietly zooming out into the hall to continue its nightly duties.

I turned up the volume, needing to hear what was being said, though part of me dreaded it. The screen showed a police chief standing amidst a throng of officers and flashing lights outside the Callahan building's main entrance.

"We have reason to believe that James and Samantha Callahan were involved in unauthorized and highly dangerous robotics experiments," the chief announced. "These experiments included the creation of advanced AI units designed to mimic human behavior. It is suspected they used illegal brain scans to enhance their technology, leading to potentially life-threatening side effects. We are only now uncovering the extent of their medical testing scam."

The camera panned back to the studio, where a serious-looking reporter picked up the story. "It has been revealed that

Aria Callahan was a robot replacement for the real Mrs. Callahan who passed away several years ago. The sophisticated Callabot is believed to have been destroyed tonight in a police raid at the Callahan building. In a heartbreaking twist, it has also been suggested that the Callahans' own child, Kieran Callahan, may not be what he seems. While details are still emerging, there are unconfirmed reports from sources close to the Callahan family suggesting that Kieran himself may be a product of these unethical experiments—a highly advanced AI, created to replace or mimic their real son, who some say may have died after a tragic accident several years ago."

My heart pounded as I listened, the implications sinking in.

The camera shifted to an image of Kieran, a recent school photo, his face innocent and smiling.

"The fate of Kieran Callahan is now under intense scrutiny. The boy has been missing since police rescued him from what can only be described as a hostage situation in Samantha Callahan's office. Child welfare authorities and robotics experts are reportedly debating whether this android, designed with the likeness and possibly the memories of a real child, should be dismantled or preserved for study. The decision could set a precedent for the future of AI and robotics, but many are questioning whether a robot, no matter how advanced, can truly be considered a 'child'—and if so, what rights it should be afforded. He was last seen with three unidentified adults who have since disappeared."

The report cut to an interview with a child welfare advocate, her face grave.

"This situation is unprecedented," she said. "If Kieran is indeed a robot, we must consider what is best for him. Does he have a future outside of Callahan, Inc.? Should he be allowed to integrate into society, or is it too dangerous? And what of the moral implications of allowing a machine to exist under the guise of a human child?"

The camera returned to the reporter, her voice softer now, more reflective. "As authorities grapple with these questions, one thing is clear: Kieran Callahan's fate hangs in the balance. The world is watching, and whatever decision is made could have far-reaching consequences—not just for him, but for the very definition of what it means to be human."

My grip tightened on the remote as the report concluded, the image of Kieran's innocent face lingering on the screen. The thought of him being dismantled, treated like a mere machine, gnawed at me. I thought back to the time I'd spent with Kieran, moments that felt so real, so human. And I remembered how much Aria had cared for him, how fiercely she'd protected him.

In that moment, my fears resolved. The horror I had felt when Kieran had been exposed as a robot, rather than a boy, melted away, replaced by a protective instinct I couldn't ignore. Would I really let Kieran fall into the hands of those who would strip him down to circuits and wires? I had already lost Aria—another connection to Meredith, destroyed. Did I want to lose whatever Meredith had entrusted to Kieran, whatever she wanted me to know?

At that moment, I knew for certain: I was taking Kieran home.

CHAPTER 28
BACK ON THE RANCH

Six months later...

KIERAN RODE the ATV in the open field closest to the house, a wide smile plastered across his face as he carved large circles into the earth. Mud sprayed up in arcs, splattering the jeans I'd pulled fresh from the wash that morning. Spring had arrived in Kemper Creek, and with it came a sense of renewal, a rebirth that seemed to breathe life back into the old homestead. This was what the ranch had needed all along. I could see that now.

"Time to come in for lunch!" I called out from the barn, with Spark trotting by my side. The old border collie had shown up a few days after I'd returned home with Kieran, riding in Katrina's rundown sedan. She'd waved off any talk of repayment, claiming she was about to buy something new, anyway. I'd been happy to let it go, more focused on settling back into a life I hoped would be normal again.

The thugs James Callahan had sent to tear apart my house must've scared Spark, but he'd found his way back—thankfully. He wasn't used to strangers invading his territory, and neither was I. Seeing him trot back up to the front porch was one of the best sights of my life. Spark had taken to Kieran instantly, as if he'd figured out the boy needed something to ground him.

"Aw, just a few more minutes?" Kieran's voice drifted back as he slowed the ATV, then turned in my direction. "Mom would've let me," he added with a cheeky grin.

A familiar sadness overcame me at the mention of Meredith—or, rather, the memories of her that still lived inside Kieran. Spark, ever sensitive, nudged his head under my hand, whining softly. Without thinking, I scratched his ears, a reflex as old as the bond between man and dog. "She probably would have," I muttered, knowing Kieran had won the argument before he even turned the ATV back toward the furthest reaches of the field.

At first, it had been disconcerting—disturbing even—the way Kieran seemed to know things about Meredith, things no child his age should know. But I understood why. The long drive home from Chicago to Idaho had given me endless hours to ask him questions. About Meredith, her work, and the secrets she'd hidden away in my marble.

Kieran had explained it all with the precision of someone far beyond his years. My wife's expertise in robotics, the breakthrough in code that had made her creations so lifelike they were indistinguishable from humans—except this code, this gift, now existed in only one place: Kieran's mind. Meredith had made sure to destroy her work at Callahan, Inc. and at the university. Disguised as a member of Turing's Acolytes, she had convinced them to raid the library archives at Northwestern's Mudd Library and wipe away every trace of her research.

But why? Why had she decided to destroy her own legacy? The story she'd told me through Kieran still haunted me...

．．．

"James and I married right after my college graduation. He seemed dashing, handsome—and rich. Samantha and I were best friends, and marrying her brother felt like the perfect fit. But as time went on, James changed. He became controlling, jealous, mean. By then, I was already pregnant and determined to make the marriage work. I thought giving him a son would soften him, make him more loving.

When Kieran was small, I took him to visit my aunt outside the city. On the way, we were hit by a truck driven by a robot. I woke up in the hospital to find my son barely clinging to life. James blamed me, even though the robot driver was found to be severely out of maintenance. But that didn't matter. I still felt the guilt—after all, I'd been the one driving. The doctors told us to make peace with losing him, but I couldn't. Neither could James.

He was our boy. Our precious son.

Then I had a radical idea: I could bring him back. If only—

That day, I set on a course to relieve my guilt, to soothe my grief. I told James I could build us a replacement—a robot so perfect, so lifelike, we wouldn't be able to tell the difference. He was immediately on board, and for the first time in months, he seemed to love me again.

Not long after Kieran died, I began creating a new Kieran. We had so many videos, pictures, and memories that I could use as the foundation for his personality. I decided to build him as an older boy, someone we would have known if he'd lived. The boy we both thought we deserved to have.

And yet, even as I started to recreate Kieran, I couldn't stop thinking about the accident. A robot had taken my son from me, and it had only happened because its programming couldn't adapt to the unpredictable movements of traffic. Robots couldn't think or react like humans. I wanted to change that. I wanted to create something better—a robot that could learn, process, and adjust in real time. I poured that passion into my work, hoping that, somehow, it would mean no one else would have to suffer the way we had. But instead of bringing James and me closer, my work became something darker. He saw my creation as perfection—a way to control his world—and I realized too late that he would never see Kieran as more than a possession."

Kieran's voice echoed in my mind, the boy's uncanny understanding of his origins rattling me all over again. This wasn't some abstract story. This was real, this was my life. My wife had built the boy who was in the field, riding the ATV, laughing as if nothing was wrong.

And yet...

Spark barked, pulling me from my thoughts. I glanced up, watching Kieran make another wide loop before heading back toward me. His laughter carried on the spring breeze, carefree, full of life. But behind that laughter was something more—a depth that wasn't quite human.

As I stood there, the sun casting long shadows across the field, I understood Kieran could never be the boy Meredith and James had wanted him to be. She'd known it, but James couldn't accept it. She'd fled Chicago realizing what a mistake she'd made in her grief and sorrow. It had been wrong to create such a realistic human and the knowledge of how to build such a thing had to be destroyed.

But Kieran held Meredith's memories inside him, and I was unwilling to lose that connection. She'd built this creature with love and grief. How could I not care for him?

A distant rumble of thunder interrupted my thoughts,

drawing my attention to the horizon. Dark clouds were rolling in fast.

"Kieran!" I called out. "Storm's coming. Time to head in."

He waved back, his grin undimmed by the looming weather.

As he sped toward me, I felt the weight of the future settle on my shoulders. There was so much I still didn't know—so much I wasn't sure I wanted to know.

But one thing was certain: Kieran wasn't just a machine.

And neither was his story over.

As we sat at the kitchen table where Meredith and I had shared so many meals, I set half a peanut butter and jelly sandwich down in front of Kieran. I didn't know the first thing about how Kieran was put together—even though the schematics were inside his head, ready for download at any time—but I figured out he liked to eat at least a few bites. That much was clear. He'd told me since the beginning he'd take care of any sanitary needs, so I trusted him on that one.

"Can I ride the ATV some more after lunch, Uncle Eli?" He swung his legs under the table, brimming with energy, barely able to sit still.

I'd asked him to call me "Uncle" when we stopped at our first gas station on the drive back from Chicago. It made things easier to explain, especially to strangers.

Spark rested his head in Kieran's lap. The sight of it—of the boy and dog together—would've made Meredith so happy.

At that moment, the rain started to fall. Big, heavy drops. The kind that turned everything outside into a thick, sticky mess during what we Idahoans liked to call 'mud season.'

"I think you'll have to wait until everything dries out," I

said, sitting down beside him. I bit into my own sandwich, hunger gnawing at me after a long morning of cleaning out the barn. I sometimes had Kieran help with chores, but most days, I preferred letting him run wild on the ranch, doing what nine-year-old ranch boys should be doing.

"But..." he protested, glancing out the window at the muddy field.

"You'll have all summer to ride around out there," I reassured him, taking a sip of milk from the glass beside my plate. "Why don't we do something indoors this afternoon? How about a slide show?"

Kieran's eyes lit up. He loved being the projector for me, showing me the countless videos and slides his mother had stored in the prism drive. Some were academic—we usually skipped those—but others were filled with memories, like family vacations or afternoons spent by the lakeshore. We always avoided the ones with James. Kieran would frown whenever his father appeared on screen, swiping past the images without hesitation. I wasn't sure why Meredith had included them in the drive, but I suppose she could've been in a hurry when she made the device.

I loved looking at the photos of Meredith from her younger years, the days before I met her. Back then, she was always smiling, making silly faces, happy. By the time I'd come into her life, a sadness had settled into her. But seeing those moments from her past warmed something deep inside me. Maybe that's why she had created the marble and left it for me—so I wouldn't feel so alone.

"Yes! Let's do a slide show." Kieran hopped up and took his plate to the sink like I'd taught him. Then, with a skip in his step, he headed into the living room. "Hurry up, Uncle Eli!"

I smiled as I carried my dishes to the sink, watching him set up his position in front of the blank wall next to the piano—his favorite spot for his shows. "This time, can you tell me about her last trip to Chicago?" I asked.

We'd already gone through a lot of Meredith's history, but I'd avoided digging too much into the later years. It was still painful for me, knowing she'd been lying to me about her trips to the city. The truth behind those visits was a question I wasn't sure I wanted answered.

Just as I was about to join Kieran, my phone rang. I unrolled it and was surprised by the number flashing on the screen.

"Katrina? I didn't expect to hear from you again." We'd last spoken was six months ago, when she'd handed me the keys to her beat-up car and pointed me toward the back roads that would avoid most of the police checkpoints. Somehow, I'd managed to get Kieran out of the city without being identified, despite all the cameras in that alley where we'd seen Aria for the last time. I had my suspicions that Officer Watts had played a part in covering our tracks, but I'd never be sure.

"He's out." Katrina's voice was tense.

"Who's out?" I asked, confusion rippling through me.

"James Callahan," she replied, her voice barely above a whisper.

"They gave him bail?" I asked, incredulous. The last I'd heard, he'd been denied release due to his flight risk—after all, he had access to his own private jet, not to mention his father's deep pockets to replace the frozen assets.

"House arrest," she said. "Just this afternoon. It'll probably be all over the news."

I walked into the living room where Kieran was waiting, ready to project the slides. His inquisitive gaze met mine. "I thought we were going to do the slide show?" he asked, a touch of disappointment in his voice.

"One minute," I said, waving my hand toward the holographic television. It flickered on.

"What's happening?" Kieran joined me near the screen.

Navigating to the main news station, I pulled up the report Katrina had mentioned. The headline blared across the screen: *James Callahan Released on House Arrest.*

"You think we're in danger?" I asked Katrina, my stomach tightening as I looked at Kieran.

"I don't know," Katrina replied. "But I'm worried. If he can get out of jail after all this time, what else is he capable of?"

———

It is said that sheepherding is one of the loneliest occupations. A Basque sheepherder could spend months alone with his flock on the desolate and unforgiving landscape of the American West, where the land itself seemed to resist habitation. In winter, he would settle in the low-lying deserts to escape the heavy snowfalls, and then in summer, he would drive the herd into the lush meadows of the Sawtooth Mountains. But eventually, as grazing practices changed and laws brought public lands under federal control, many Basques began buying ranches to continue the work they'd grown to love. They'd return to their homeland to find wives, and gradually, tight-knit communities took root in the American soil.

The Zurbano family was no different. My grandfather told me the stories his grandfather had passed down to him—stories of how they transformed from isolated herders, barely knowing English, into proud ranch owners and family men. But in the last forty years or so, Basque sheep ranchers had become a rare breed. When I used what little of the language I remembered—*kaixo, mesedez,* and *eskerrik asko*—most folks would give me strange looks, as if I'd lost my mind. But in Kemper Creek, if you looked hard enough, you could still find a few old-timers who'd smile at the old language, give a knowing nod, and share a secret look. They understood, just as I did: we are Basque.

My whole life, I'd felt like an outsider in this town. Sure, I'd made friends, like John, but I always kept a distance. My parents and their parents before them had taught us to stick to family, to be resilient and self-reliant. Depend on no one but yourself.

That created a certain mindset in a man. When his wife or child was threatened, he acted differently than someone who felt he had a community to lean on in difficult times.

When Katrina told me James Callahan had been placed on house arrest, I knew he would come for me. Somehow, he'd pulled strings to get out of prison before his trial, and the slow-burning fire in my gut told me he was out for revenge.

His lackeys had already come to my home and tossed it upside down. He knew exactly where I lived, and I had no doubt he figured out Kieran was with me. Where else would he be? For weeks after the Callahan arrests, the news had been dominated by the story of the mysterious Kieran Callahan—the robot boy who'd fooled everyone. His friends, his teachers—no one had suspected a thing. The principal of the Balfour Day School had been one of the first to be interviewed. Pale-faced and visibly shaken, she told the press that Kieran had enrolled the year before and that his mother had explained he'd been homeschooled—a common story among the elite. The principal had been in shock the whole time, her expression slack, her eyes vacant as she described the lovely young mother, Aria, and her delightfully bright son, Kieran. Never once did she suspect that either of them could have been highly advanced robots—machines capable of far more than she could ever imagine.

But no one had been able to locate Kieran. The last time he was seen was at the Callahan building and the police had been so busy with the detention of the Callahans and their thugs and cleaning up after the robot melee, they hadn't remembered much about the frightened boy wrapped in an emergency blanket. Despite ransacking the luxury penthouse in their search, all the authorities had found were pieces and parts of an older model robot, none of which contained the advanced tech found in the Callabots. Though the older model seemed outdated and less sophisticated, it was still shipped off to be destroyed like all the others. Anything with the Callahan name had become the new boogeyman.

Kemper Creek was among the few places left in the world where people didn't pay much attention to the news beyond their own lives. Kieran's photo had been spread across the country, sent as alerts on every phone within a five-hundred-mile radius of Chicago. But we'd escaped the city on that first day of driving—well before the authorities had pieced together the facts—and by the time they did, we were far beyond their reach. Six months later, the frenzy had died down. Now, only the occasional news feature brought up Kieran's name, mostly focusing on the dark revelations about the illegal brain scans that powered the Callabots. Workers at the company were coming forward, begging for mercy and light sentences, claiming they had no idea the scans were causing cancer or that people's memories had been stolen to build the AI systems that made the robots so eerily human.

Where once people lined up to work for Callahan, Inc., these days the name sparked nothing but anger and disgust.

Victims and their families filed lawsuits, only to learn that the company's assets had been frozen by the feds.

Yes, James would come for me and Kieran. That much was obvious. I'd prepared for this moment for months, mentally checking off tasks, knowing a few more still remained if I wanted to feel secure when James came knocking.

But tonight, I wanted to enjoy a simple slide show with Kieran. One last night to pretend everything was normal. I rolled up my phone after hanging up with Katrina and tucked it into the front pocket of my jeans, right next to my marble—where it belonged. Even though all the data it contained now lived inside Kieran, the marble reminded me of Meredith and everything I'd gone through to uncover her secrets. It was proof that she had lived. Proof that I had loved her. Proof that I would never forget any of it.

I sat down on the couch, put my feet up on the coffee table, and turned to Kieran. "What are you going to show me tonight?" I asked, trying to keep my voice steady, as though nothing had changed.

But in the back of my mind, I knew that after tonight, nothing would ever be simple again.

THE NEXT EVENING, the wind carried a warmer touch than the chill of the day before. Spring came late to this part of the world. Where flower beds in other states had already sprung to life and trees budded with fresh green, in Idaho, the landscape was slower to awaken. Kieran and I sat on the porch, watching the road that curved around the edge of my ranch. His young eyes were sharper than mine, and I'd asked him to let me know if he saw anyone coming.

"Uncle Eli," Kieran said, interrupting my thoughts as I sipped from a sweating glass of lemonade. He pointed to the northeast, where a faint rumble reached my ears.

"What do you see?" I asked, standing and squinting into the late afternoon light.

"A car. A fancy one."

James Callahan. It didn't take him long to find a way out of his penthouse prison. He must've convinced one of his hired hands to wear the ankle monitor in his place. Home detention tech hadn't improved much over the years, and Callahan had never met a rule he couldn't break.

I whistled for Spark, who lay resting on the porch beside

me. His ears perked up at the sound, and he stirred. The old border collie wagged his tail, struggling to rise to his feet. I hoped he still had it in him for what I needed him to do. I added a second whistle, one he knew well, and Spark trotted off toward the pasture where the ewes and their lambs were penned. Most had given birth in the past month—tiny and fragile, but perfect for creating chaos when spooked.

"It's getting closer," Kieran said, his voice tense.

I glanced up and saw the sleek black air car now visible to the naked eye. Its dark four-door frame stood out against the landscape, as it hovered above the pavement. Even from this distance, I could make out three silhouettes inside—James wouldn't come alone.

"Time for you to hide." I gave Kieran a gentle nudge toward the house. He'd slip out the back and head up the hill, where a hidden cave nestled into the rocky outcroppings provided a perfect vantage point and kept him out of harm's way.

"I don't like hiding," he said, frustration coloring his voice.

"I know." I ruffled his hair.

He paused, looking at me. "I could help. I want to help."

"Your mother would want you safe," I replied, leaving no room for argument.

The screen door slammed shut behind him, and I watched him disappear inside. He'd reach the cave I'd scouted in less than five minutes. No one would think to search for him up there.

I grabbed my father's old rifle, which leaned against the porch railing, and secured it on the back of the ATV parked outside the barn. This morning, I'd packed the gear I'd need, fully expecting this moment to come. I'd spent hours setting up surprises along the canyon—James and his men wouldn't find this chase as simple as they expected. I revved the engine and shot off to the furthest reaches of the ranch, away from the house and into the canyon, where the land stretched for miles. Out there, cell signals and Wi-Fi couldn't reach. James was about to get a lesson in wilderness survival.

As I sped past the sheep pen, I whistled one more time. Spark sprang into action, using his nose to unlatch the gate, as he'd done hundreds of times before. I thought Spark was too old for this kind of work, but he proved me wrong when I needed him most.

The gate swung open, and the ewes and lambs flooded into the larger front pasture, their white wool stark against the dark earth. A hundred skittish sheep with newborns to protect would throw any pursuit into chaos. James's air car was nearly at the driveway now. I zoomed past the barn, unlatched the gate near the far entrance, and then sped out into the muddy field. The grass was just starting to green, but the ground was still slick from the recent thaw. I left the gate wide open, knowing exactly what would happen next.

Spark, slower these days, did his best to catch up with me. In his prime, he would've been at my heels in no time, jumping onto the rear of the ATV as we raced across the fields. But now, his gray muzzle and stiff joints made the chase a struggle. I slowed, glancing over my shoulder to see the black air car veer off the road and start following my trail, clearly trying to keep up. The uneven terrain wasn't as easy for an air car to glide over.

"Come on, Spark." I slapped my thigh, encouraging him as he lumbered closer. His breathing was labored, but he didn't seem to care. When he finally reached me, I slowed enough for him to attempt a leap onto the back. I caught his rear end and lifted him aboard.

With Spark safely behind me, I tore across the muddy

pasture, sticking close to the fence line where the ground was firmer. Every year, since I was a boy, I'd learned the patterns of this land, the dry patches and hidden dips that would trip up anyone unfamiliar with it. As I led James deeper into the canyon, further from the house and Kieran, I hoped I could end this here and now.

My pulse quickened as I thought of the final piece of my plan. Kieran would be safe by now, hidden in the cave. I tightened my grip on the handlebars and scanned the canyon. James was coming, and he wouldn't stop until one of us fell.

This wasn't only about survival, it was about finishing what Meredith started—or this all would've been for nothing.

The minute James swung his heavy air car into the field, the trouble began. Built for city streets and sleek highways, his vehicle wasn't designed for off-roading. I glanced over my shoulder, gunning the ATV forward. The scattered sheep created perfect obstacles, forcing the car to swerve and slow. Behind me, the car had trouble stabilizing over the mud but, to my dismay, it hit a patch of turf and managed to regain its forward motion. I swore under my breath and refocused. Time for step two.

I veered toward the marshy area where spring rains had turned the ground into a deceptive quagmire. I knew this terrain like the back of my hand. The mud here was deep and sticky—and hopefully would compromise the air car.

We entered a narrow strip of dry land James's vehicle wouldn't fit through. As I passed, I lured him onto the spit of land running alongside the mud pit. From a distance, it looked like a lush meadow, its grass bright and green thanks to the thaw. But looks were deceiving. Lambs had been fooled by this very spot many times, lured into the mud by the promising grass only to get stuck until I could free them.

Now James fell into the same trap. His car floated over the hidden mud, then lost stability. The rear end tilted wildly and one corner sank deep into the muck. Mud splattered everywhere as he slammed the accelerator, trying to free himself. All he succeeded in doing was burying the car deeper.

I idled my ATV at a safe distance, watching. I knew this wouldn't stop them, but it would slow them down, make them come to me on foot. And they would. James hadn't come all this way to negotiate. He was out for blood—driven by the fact a simple sheep rancher had dismantled his empire, taken his son, and exposed what he'd done to his wife. It wasn't just rage; it was a kind of cold, calculating hatred that only a man like James Callahan could muster.

Three car doors flew open. James emerged first, followed by the bald enforcer I remembered from Chicago and another thug built like a linebacker. They wouldn't find the traps I'd laid as easy to avoid on foot as they might in their fancy car.

James struggled through the mud toward the trunk, each step a monumental effort, before pausing to glare at me. Our eyes locked, and even from that distance, I could feel the fury radiating off him. This was a man who'd scanned Meredith's brain, knowing it would kill her, and he wouldn't hesitate to do worse to me.

I waited and watched, scratching Spark's ears as he wagged his tail beside me. My old dog didn't have any idea what we were up to, but he trusted me, and I trusted him. I wanted to know what we'd be up against.

The bald enforcer reached the trunk first, hauling out what looked like a top-of-the-line Callahan herding drone. The other thug extracted something I couldn't quite make out, but the metallic glint set my nerves on edge. James stayed by the car, focused on his phone. All three spread out, and I knew it was time to move.

The drone buzzed toward me like a vulture, low and fast. I knew enough about herding drones to understand the danger—John Tellman had once tried to sell me on them, boasting about their capabilities. Beyond tracking livestock, they could deliver tranquilizer darts, deploy cattle prods, or even capture nets.

Spark barked furiously as the drone closed in, so I accelerated, weaving through a grove of quaking aspens just beginning to sprout their new leaves. I hoped the trees would confuse the drone, but James had anticipated that. It rose high above them and swooped down to meet me on the other side.

It was faster than I expected, keeping pace as I zigzagged through the terrain. I could hear the high-pitched whine of its motors, a sound that set my teeth on edge. Up ahead, the canyon narrowed—my sanctuary. I called it the Dead Zone because no signal ever worked there. Meredith used to hate it; she liked to stay connected and text me when I was out alone. But I'd always loved it. It was my own private escape, where the outside world couldn't touch me. And now the Dead Zone was going to save me, if I could make it there in time.

The drone followed close behind, its cattle prod deployed, sparking as it closed in. I swerved, dodging the attack, but I was out of cover. The drone buzzed only feet from me, and I ducked instinctively. It sailed over me, then suddenly twisted mid-air, spiraled, and slammed into the canyon wall. The explosion sent burning fragments raining down. A piece of shrapnel struck my ATV's front tire, and I was launched into the air.

In the brief moment before I hit the ground, I had only one thought: "Where are you, Spark?"

I WOKE up with my head pounding, disoriented, lying on the wet ground. The world around me was blurry, and I had no idea how long I'd been out. A wet tongue licked my face.

"Spark," I muttered, trying to reach up to pet him. But the excruciating pain in my shoulder stopped me cold. Agony radiated down my arm, up through my collarbone, and even into my back and chest. Every breath felt tight, and lowering my hand, even by a fraction, sent stabbing pain through me.

I'd messed myself up pretty good. Probably broke something.

Dammit.

With a groan, I managed to sit up, the world tilting. My mangled ATV lay crumpled a few yards away, a twisted wreck. I could only assume Spark had managed to jump clear of the crash faster than I had. Thank God my dog seemed unharmed.

Spark whined, nudging my side, and I reached out with my good left hand to pet him, trying to calm him—and myself. "What next, Spark?" I asked through gritted teeth, struggling to get to my feet. A sharp pain in my shoulder flared again, nearly knocking me back down. I had no time for this. I had to move, had to end this before James got any closer. The pain could wait. It had to.

First things first. I needed to stabilize my shoulder. I pulled off my belt and fashioned a crude sling, looping it around my neck to prop up my arm. It wasn't comfortable—far from it—but at least it stopped some of the pain and gave me a little more clarity. I grabbed the small pack I'd strapped to the ATV and unhooked my dad's old rifle. I'd never shot it left-handed, but I might not have a choice. Against three determined men, it wasn't much, but it was better than nothing.

My mind raced through the traps I'd laid out before James arrived. The terrain itself was my first ally—the narrow canyon would force them to come at me one at a time. But I'd added insurance. Just ahead, concealed under branches and leaves, lay the first trap—a ten-foot pit lined with sharpened stakes. Spark and I had spent hours making sure the covering would hold our weight near the edges but collapse under a direct step. The second trap waited higher up—a carefully balanced collection of logs that one pull of a rope would send cascading down.

I hated it might come to this—these weren't the kind of traps meant for survival. But James had forced my hand. If he'd only let Kieran go, accepted his arrest... I pushed the thought away. I'd do what needed to be done.

I walked through the creek that snaked through the canyon floor, the cold water numbing my ankles. Spark stayed close, understanding the gravity of our situation. We picked our way carefully around the covered pit, using the path we'd marked with subtle scratches on rocks. From here, I could spot the perfect vantage point to watch the trap's effectiveness.

Concealed behind a boulder, I heard them before I saw them. The bald bodyguard led the way, followed by the line-backer-built thug. James brought up the rear, his expensive shoes already ruined by the creek bed. I held my breath as they approached the pit.

The bald man paused, studying the ground, but his partner pushed past impatiently. Two steps, and the covering gave way. The man disappeared into the pit. His scream echoed off the canyon walls, cut short by a sickening thud.

"Help me!" His voice was thick with pain. "Oh God, please."

My body tensed. I knew what lay in wait for him at the bottom. I tried to blank out my imagination and the dark vision of the man's body impaled on the sharp sticks. I had to do this for Kieran. It was the only way.

The bald enforcer moved to help, but James's cold voice stopped him. "Leave him. Zurbano's close—I can feel it."

"But sir—"

"Move."

I used their distraction to slip away, working my way up to the second trap's trigger point. Spark waited faithfully below in a stay position behind a few clumps of sagebrush. The pain in my shoulder made climbing difficult and a few times I thought I'd lose my grip on the sharp rocks, but adrenaline pushed me forward. I'd barely reached the right position, about fifteen feet above the canyon floor, when I heard a mechanical whir.

The bald enforcer had pulled something from his pack— sleek, metallic, with a digital display glowing orange. A Crop-Guard 5000, Callahan's latest in pest control technology. It could track heat signatures through walls, delivering a lethal nerve agent meant for burrowing rodents. In human targets... I didn't want to think about it.

The device hummed to life, its sensor already turning toward my hiding place. I had seconds to act. With feet tightly jammed into the canyon face, I yanked the rope with my good arm, and the logs thundered down the canyon wall. The remaining bodyguard looked up too late. The logs plowed into him full force and bounced over his body, burying him in thousands of pounds of lumber. He didn't even have time to yell before he was crushed beneath them. An arm sticking out of the pile, bloody and mangled, was the only sign of him.

The CropGuard 5000 quickly lost altitude without its handler and landed at an angle on top of the logs, its whirring blades slowing down until they stopped altogether.

The silence that followed was broken only by the creek's gentle burble. Even the man in the pit had gone quiet.

James's voice carried up to me, tight with fury but tinged with something else. Fear? "It's just you and me now, Zurbano." The logs had also blocked his path into the canyon, giving me time to make a getaway.

I turned my attention to the terrain. The end of the narrow canyon ahead was my best bet. If I could make it through the bottleneck, I might have a chance to pick off James before he even saw me. I waded through the creek and sloshed toward the steep walls rising on either side.

In my mind, I played out the old westerns my dad had loved, imagining how men used the land as their weapon. This canyon would be mine. James was alone now, but that might make him even more dangerous. A man with nothing left to lose is a different kind of threat. I had to make it work.

The pack slung over my good shoulder was heavier than it should've been, weighed down with a hydration-protein gummy pack, a few essentials like a slingshot, and a small first-aid kit. But that wasn't what mattered. I had to reach higher ground.

I reached an outcropping I'd scouted, about twenty-five feet up. It was a grueling climb, especially with one arm out of commission. More than once, my boots slipped on the loose gravel, and I had to brace myself against the rocks, cursing the pain every time I did. But I couldn't stop. Not now.

By the time I reached the top, Spark had already trotted ahead, waiting for me, tail wagging as if this was any other day, as if we hadn't just watched two men die. I collapsed onto the flat ledge beside him, out of breath, my shoulder screaming. But I'd made it.

The narrow entrance to the canyon was below me and the dead end farther down to the south, where James would be trapped. I settled into the cover of a cluster of junipers, rifle resting against the rocks. Now, it was a waiting game.

As I scanned the canyon, my thoughts turned to Kieran. James would never let his "son" go so easily. Kieran was too important, too valuable. And with his empire crumbling, his men dead in my canyon, Kieran was all James had left. That would make him unpredictable.

However, I'd trained the boy well. I'd told him if I ever instructed him to hide in the cave, he wasn't to come out until either I or Spark came for him.

But that didn't stop me from worrying. James was like a bulldog when it came to things he believed he owned. He had supported Meredith's idea to create Kieran as a replacement for their dead human son, which was a twisted attempt to reclaim what he'd lost. James had wanted Kieran to look like and act like a boy—a boy who would never grow up, never challenge him, never leave him.

To me, Kieran was more than a robotic facsimile of a child. He was Meredith's final creation, her masterpiece. The Callabots were cheap imitations, flawed versions of what she had once envisioned. Even Aria, with her ability to break commands and think for herself, wasn't truly Meredith's. Only Kieran carried her genius, her vision.

That's why I had to take care of him, no matter what. Do my best to keep him functioning, to protect him at all costs. Because Kieran was a part of Meredith. He was all I had left of her, and I'd protect him with my life.

I adjusted my makeshift sling, trying to find a position that didn't send waves of pain through my shoulder. From this vantage, I could see everything.

The shadows lengthened as the sun dipped lower. I tightened my grip on my rifle firmly, waiting, watching.

Then, Spark growled low, a signal that James had entered the canyon.

My heart pounded, echoing the throbbing ache in my shoulder.

I awkwardly adjusted the rifle, squinting through the fading light.

I had a chance to take Callahan out. Did I have the guts to do it?

AS I WAS ABOUT to pull the trigger, Spark's growl evolved into a full, thunderous bark. The sound ricocheted off the surrounding canyon walls like a warning shot of its own. James swung his head in my direction, and our gazes locked. My left index finger twitched.

The rifle went off. The shot cracked through the air, but I missed my target by a wide margin. The bullet buried itself in the dirt two feet above Callahan's head.

Dammit.

Even the small recoil from the .22 sent a fresh surge of pain through my injured shoulder, as though someone had driven a hot nail through it. My grip faltered, and I dropped the rifle. It tumbled off the edge of the ridge, clattering against the rocky outcrop before coming to rest just beyond my reach.

Spark, who had never met a stranger he didn't like, let out a growl so feral it sent chills down my spine. I'd never heard him do that before, not in all the years he'd been by my side. With a speed that surprised me, Spark shot down the steep trail toward James, teeth bared.

"Spark, no!" I called after him.

I scrambled to my feet, ignoring the searing pain in my shoulder. But Spark was already too far ahead. As I watched him close in on Callahan, everything seeming to slow down around me. My dog leapt through the air with an energy I hadn't seen in years, his powerful frame aimed directly at James.

James raised his arm to shield his face before Spark collided with him. There was a sickening sound as James's boot swung, connecting with Spark's right front leg midair. The dog yelped —a high-pitched sound that cut through me—and tumbled onto a patch of loose gravel near the stream.

He lay still.

A fury ignited in me, a blaze of anger that burned away every other thought. My vision blurred. Without hesitation, I sprinted down the slope, my boots skidding on the uneven rocks. The ground gave way beneath me more than once, but I didn't care. The only thing I knew was James Callahan had to pay—for my wife, for Spark, for everything he'd taken from me.

Each step sent jolts of pain through my damaged shoulder, but I shoved the agony aside, pushing through it. Callahan had stolen Meredith's life with that cursed brain scan. Now he'd come for my dog, too. My hesitation from up on the ridge disappeared. I didn't care what the cost would be. I wanted him gone. For good.

I reached the bottom of the slope faster than I thought possible, launching myself at James with all the force I could muster. The two of us tumbled into the icy creek, the cold water a shocking jolt that drove the breath from my lungs. My arm came free of its sling, and though the agony in my shoulder was excruciating, I forced both hands around James's throat.

I didn't know if I had the strength to crush his windpipe, but I was damn sure going to try.

"You killed Meredith," I growled between gritted teeth, tightening my grip with each word. "What did she ever do to you? Why?"

James's eyes bulged, his face contorting as he gasped for air. His fingers clawed at mine, trying to pry them away, but I held firm. I could feel the desperation in his movements as he bucked beneath me, trying to throw me off.

The pain in my shoulder wracked me, my muscles trembling as my strength began to falter. James took advantage of the moment and with a savage twist, rolled me off of him. I fell back into the creek, my back slamming against the cold, slick stones. The current washed over me, soaking my clothes and chilling me to the bone.

"She killed my son," James spat, his voice raw with fury. "That bitch killed my son. You think you've suffered? You don't know a damn thing about loss."

He drove his fist into my face, and my head snapped back. My vision blurred as a sharp ringing filled my ears, but I could still hear his voice, dripping with venom.

"The only thing she ever did right was build Kieran. The boy he could've been if it weren't for her recklessness."

James's hands gripped the front of my shirt, lifting me just enough to slam my head against the rocks beneath the water. My skull cracked against the stone, and the world around me grew dim.

"I want her code," he hissed, his face inches from mine. "I want her work. She stole it from me and gave it to you—a redneck idiot who doesn't even know the difference between a circuit and a fuse. Nobody steals from a Callahan."

With another violent slam, my head hit the rock once more, and the darkness began to close in, swallowing the edges of my vision. The cold water lapped at my face as my body went limp. I could feel myself slipping away, the icy stream pulling me down into its depths.

"I'm sorry, Meredith," I whispered, the words barely audible over the rushing water. "I'm sorry..."

My face sank beneath the cold stream...

CHAPTER 32
KIERAN

THE WALK through the field had been interesting. Kieran had never traveled so far on foot before. Usually, he and Uncle Eli rode the ATVs if they were going more than a short walk from home. The inside gate stood wide open, and the ewes with their lambs had spread out over the muddy field, nibbling at fresh shoots of grass that had sprung up in the last few weeks.

Although his uncle had instructed him to stay hidden in the cave, Kieran couldn't shake the worry gnawing at him. Hours had passed since the dark air car had pulled up the driveway and followed Uncle Eli into the field. To distract himself, he sifted through the vast data his mother had left him—his real mother. Not the android version his father had created to fill the gap.

He remembered the real Aria. Her warm smile, her gentle touch, the life that sparkled in her blue eyes when she'd powered him up for the first time. She probably hadn't realized how clearly he would remember that moment, but he did. To go from nothing to everything in an instant had been amazing. Lights, sounds, sensations—all flooding his circuits at once. He had relished the rush of data filling the emptiness within him, like the satisfaction of eating after a long hunger.

For a while, it had only been the two of them, alone in a room. He understood now it had been a lab in the Callahan building, a locked space where she worked tirelessly, perfecting every intricate detail. Sometimes she cried. Sometimes she held him close and whispered how much she loved him. And other times, she worked in silence, her focus on the delicate wires or precise lines of code she quietly tweaked.

Kieran trudged through the mud, following the distinctive tire tracks of the ATV. The marks it left in the mud were unmistakable—easy for him to track.

When Kieran had first been brought to the high-rise penthouse, his father had been thrilled to meet him. The look of delight on James's face had warmed Kieran's circuits. But Aria's expression had been different. Her joy had slowly transformed into sorrow during those last few weeks of tweaking his programming. Kieran realized her motivations had changed. Creating him had once fulfilled her, but over time, the result began to trouble her. And that troubled him. He had sensed her emotional distance, especially after she'd worked so hard to perfect his ability to feel emotions. Kieran understood grief, sadness, and the deep ache of a child rejected by his parent through no fault of his own. He knew he was Kieran, but not the real Kieran. And Aria could never reconcile the two.

James, however, appeared eager to move on from the real Kieran to the "improved" version. It must have been astonishing for a parent to leap from a two-year-old with a toddler's limitations to a nine-year-old boy who could converse, respond, and behave like someone far older and more advanced.

Kieran remembered how Aria would stand off to the side in their living room, her posture stiff, eyes distant, while James spent time with him. The room had large, floor-to-ceiling windows overlooking the vast blue expanse of Lake Michigan. It should have felt warm, a place of family connection, but instead, it had been filled with tension.

That autumn, James had poured his energy into Kieran, talking endlessly about his work, the people he worked with, his aspirations. Kieran absorbed it all, every word. He filed it away in his meticulously organized data banks, knowing it would be important one day. But his mother... she had grown quieter. More withdrawn.

The world never found out what happened to the real Kieran. His death had been covered up. The people involved had been paid handsomely for their silence. After all, the Callahans didn't make mistakes. The Callahans didn't suffer loss. They were rich, powerful, and, in their own eyes, perfect.

Kieran passed the air car, now stuck in the mud, and carefully skirted around the marshy area. He followed Uncle Eli's tracks further within the canyon, where the ground became rougher and wireless signals grew faint.

His sharp eyes picked out the remains of a crashed drone and the wreckage of the ATV, tangled with debris. Analyzing the scene, he calculated the trajectory of the crash and the likely injuries sustained. His concern for Uncle Eli grew.

Twenty yards ahead, an anomaly in the ground caught his attention. His sensors detected a deep depression concealed by branches and leaves—a pit trap, carefully engineered. Now he understood why Uncle Eli had been gone so long yesterday. The covering had collapsed inward, and at the bottom lay one of his father's men, impaled on sharpened stakes. Kieran's circuits processed the scene with detached efficiency, noting the precise angle of entry wounds and the statistical probability of survival: 0%.

Further along the canyon, a mass of fallen logs created another tableau of destruction. The second man lay partially visible beneath the timber, the CropGuard 5000 weapon perched atop the pile. Kieran recognized the device—one of Callahan Inc.'s more lethal agricultural innovations, repurposed for human targets.

Kieran analyzed the strategic placement of both traps, understanding the necessity of Uncle Eli's actions while calculating the escalating danger. James Callahan had lost two men but gained something perhaps more dangerous—nothing left to lose. The probability of extreme violence had increased by 78.4%.

"Uncle Eli!" he called, his voice echoing through the narrow canyon. "Where are you?"

Since entering the field, he hadn't seen a sign of his father, Uncle Eli, or even Spark. But the trail of tracks, the abandoned vehicles, and now footprints told a story. Both men were on foot, one chasing the other. Worry gnawed at him. His father's anger was something to fear, and Kieran knew James would stop at nothing to achieve his goal.

The anxiety inside him swelled, a feeling that mirrored the one he'd had the day his mother disappeared. He had called for her, desperate for her voice, but she never came. His father had offered no explanation, only an irritated glare, angrier about her absence than concerned for Kieran's loss. For days, Kieran had lain in his bed, refusing to move, plugged into his charger as he waited for her return. When his father finally brought him a robot nanny named Gwen, he had promised she would be as good, if not better, than any mother. Gwen was kind and helpful, but Kieran understood the difference. A mother wasn't something you could simply replace with an algorithm.

Kieran reached a narrow spot in the canyon where a

shallow stream flowed through. He waded into the cool water, feeling the smooth pebbles shift beneath his feet. Though Uncle Eli had told him to hide and wait, Kieran had spent the hours calculating possible outcomes. His ability to reason had grown stronger with the influx of information from his mother's brain scan. He had reached one conclusion: he had to end this. They were fighting over him, over the knowledge his mother had entrusted to him. It was only right that he have a say in how it ended.

Slipping between the narrow canyon walls, Kieran moved silently, calculating his next steps. He had almost reached the other side when the sharp crack of a gunshot echoed through the air.

CHAPTER 33
HIS CHOICE

WATER FILLED MY MOUTH, and I coughed and spluttered. Somehow, an involuntary survival instinct jolted me out of my stupor. My head broke the surface of the shallow water, and I gasped for air.

A small voice called out, clear and deliberate. "I have the code, father."

Kieran.

James's grip on my shirt loosened, and I scrambled toward the shore, coughing and clutching at the cold, rocky bank. The boy had disobeyed me—he hadn't stayed hidden in the cave like I'd told him. But as much as frustration flared, gratitude quickly followed. He had saved my life with his timely appearance.

Callahan's eyes were wide as he stared at Kieran. He hadn't expected the boy to witness this. How long had Kieran been watching? How much had he heard? James's surprise lasted only a moment before he masked it with an artificial smile.

"Kieran, come give me a hug," James said, his voice syrupy with false warmth. "I've been so worried about you. No one knew where you'd gone. I thought you were lost forever."

"Forever is an exaggeration, don't you think?" Kieran's voice was calm, but there was a hardness behind it. The nine-year-old boy was fading away, replaced by the android who carried the mind of someone far older. "You belong in jail."

James's face darkened briefly as he scanned Kieran, his eyes flickering with uncertainty. "What lies has Zurbano told you?" he asked, trying to regain control.

Kieran ignored the question and took a few slow steps forward, his gaze drifting to Spark, who lay motionless beside me. "Who hurt Spark?" The serious, calculating boy vanished, replaced by the Kieran who loved the old border collie, his features softening with concern. "He's harmless."

Kieran knelt beside Spark and gently laid a hand on the dog's chest, feeling the faint rise and fall of shallow breaths.

"He's hurt," I said, my voice heavy with concern, "but I think he'll be okay if we get him help."

"Did you do this?" Kieran's eyes met his father's.

James, still standing shin-deep in the creek, hesitated. "He lunged at me. I had no choice," he muttered, the defensive tone betraying his guilt. "He could've bitten me."

"He's old. He wouldn't have hurt you," Kieran said, rising to his feet, his posture far more adult than childlike now. His hands rested on his hips in a stance of quiet authority. "I have everything my mother hid from you—every memory, every piece of code, everything you tried to steal from her."

"Kieran," James pleaded, "I need that code. Your mother hid it from me to ruin me. You know how talented she was—she created miracles that others can't. I have to rebuild what she took from me."

I stepped forward, my voice rough with anger. "Then you shouldn't have murdered her."

"I did no such thing!" James shot back, his face flushed. "She volunteered for the brain scan. She understood the risks, and she agreed for Kieran's sake. He needed his mother. I told her if she went through with it, I'd let her go. I'd leave her alone. She wanted out of the robot business. She wanted to start fresh."

"That's a lie," I said. Memories of her summer trips to Chicago flooded back. "She had to sneak back to the city to see Kieran. Even though the android version wasn't her real son, she couldn't stay away. I understand it now. She loved him too much, even if it wasn't truly him."

Kieran looked between us, his expression unreadable. "Stop," he said, his voice cutting through the tension like a blade. "Both of you. I have all of my mother's memories. She gave them to me willingly, knowing I'd need them." His eyes narrowed at James. "I could expose the truth, father, and you know it. But I won't. You've made enough mistakes on your own, and the courts will sort it out. There's no need for me to come forward with the evidence I have inside here." He tapped the side of his head. "This is my choice. Not yours. Not Uncle Eli's. Mine."

James looked genuinely shaken. But then his hand darted to his back pocket. With a quick motion, he pulled out a stun stick.

Kieran's expression didn't change. "Don't do it, father. You'll regret it."

James flicked on the weapon, his desperation pushing him to the brink. "You're coming home with me, Kieran. One way or another."

"I have proof," Kieran said calmly, his voice carrying an authority that didn't belong to a nine-year-old. "About Callahan Inc.'s illegal brain scanning program. About the deaths. About everything."

James's hand trembled slightly, the stun stick wavering. "You're bluffing."

"Mom knew what you'd do to her. I have all of it—memory engrams, research data, surveillance footage—from the prism device you so stupidly overlooked." Kieran's eyes held his father's. "Did you really think she'd trust you with her legacy knowing the real Kieran's fate?"

I watched the color drain from James's face, my own desire for revenge warring with fascination at watching Kieran systematically dismantle his father's confidence.

"You wouldn't expose your own father," James said, but doubt had crept into his voice.

"I don't want to," Kieran agreed. "But I will if you force my hand. The neural pattern recognition software you used on those people in Chicago? Mom improved it. Made it safer. But you didn't wait for her refinements, did you? You rushed ahead, and people died." He took a step forward. "You lured her into that machine, knowing it would kill her."

James staggered as if struck. "Those are lies."

"You know I'm speaking the truth." Kieran's voice remained steady, almost gentle. "Turn yourself in, father. Face what you've done. Or I release everything—not only to the police, but to every news outlet in the country. The Callahan name will be lower than dirt, your grand legacy tarnished forever."

The stun stick slipped from James's fingers, clattering against the rocks. His shoulders slumped, his imperial bearing finally cracking. "You're exactly like her," he whispered. "Too smart for your own good."

I moved forward, kicked the weapon farther up the shore, and reached for the rope in my pack. The urge to end James Callahan still burned, but Kieran had found a better way. Justice rather than vengeance. To see his mighty empire slip from his hands and move on without him would be a lifetime of punishment. As I bound James's hands, he didn't resist. The fight had drained out of him.

"I loved you both," James said quietly. "In my own way."

"Kieran knelt beside Spark and gathered the injured dog carefully in his arms. "But love isn't ownership. Mom taught me that."

I gripped the rope's end, tugging James forward. The mighty James Callahan, reduced to trudging through the creek bed like a common prisoner. But watching Kieran cradle Spark with such tenderness, I understood what Meredith had created —not merely an advanced android, but a being capable of choosing wisdom over revenge, justice over anger.

"Doc Hardy should be in the office today," I said, falling into step beside Kieran. "We can get Spark help when we're back at the house."

Kieran nodded, his expression softening as he looked down at the dog in his arms. Without another word, we started the long walk back through the narrow canyon. And the boy who had once been the product of grief and loss had chosen his own path—one that would make his mother proud.

EPILOGUE

August 2045

IT HAD BEEN MORE than a year since James Callahan
showed up at the ranch, and life had returned to its usual
rhythm. Kieran and I barely paid attention to the news of his
father's trial. Strangely, when the police had brought James
back to Chicago, he seemed to have a miraculous change of
heart, pleading guilty to most of the charges against him. He'd
be in prison for a long time, along with his sister, though they
both ended up in minimum-security facilities. A board member
took over operation of what was left of Callahan, Inc. and insti-
tuted serious reforms under the watchful eye of the Justice
Department. That was the last I thought about them or their
company.

I sat on the porch, shucking fresh corn from the Tellman
corn patch. They grew some every summer, and this year's crop
had been a bumper one. Spark lay at my feet, his muzzle resting
on his paws. Since his recovery, Spark hadn't been the same.
His once boundless energy was gone. I often felt that day in the
canyon had been Spark's way of thanking me for a life well-

lived. So, I spoiled him. I fed him scraps from the table when Kieran wasn't looking and bought him a cushy dog bed that he slept on. He deserved it.

A delivery truck rumbled up the driveway, kicking up a cloud of late August dust. Spark lifted his head lazily but didn't move to greet it, as if it wasn't worth the effort anymore.

I set my half-shucked ear of corn aside and stood up. "Kieran, looks like we have a delivery. Did you order something?" I'd had to explain more than once that he couldn't just order parts whenever he wanted—a new spring, panel, or tool cost money. But now and then, his curiosity got the better of him. Funny how even a programmed robot could have impulses they couldn't control.

The screen door banged as Kieran stepped out onto the porch. "No, I promise."

Kieran looked the same as the day I brought him home. I didn't know why I expected him to change. Maybe it was because I'd started to see him as a real boy. The neighbors understood he was an android, as did the folks in town, and they recognized the implications if word ever got out that he was linked to the Callahans. But as long as I kept him out on the ranch, no one seemed to mind. In fact, many found pride in the fact that Meredith, a world-famous robotics expert, had chosen Kemper Creek as her home.

The truck came to a halt beside my old pickup, and the driver slid out of his seat with an awkward plop. "Got a delivery for Mr. Elijah Zurbano?" He scratched his balding head, glancing from me to Kieran.

"That's me," I said, walking down the steps. I wasn't expecting anything, but it didn't seem like an accidental order from Kieran either.

"Could you identify yourself?" The driver unrolled his

phone and pointed to a spot on the screen. I pressed my index finger into the circle, and the device confirmed my identity. "Great. Where would you like me to unload it?"

As the driver opened the back of the truck, I saw a large crate and a deactivated DeliveryBot inside. "That's the delivery?" I asked, incredulous. I hadn't ordered any new equipment. "Where did it come from?

The driver hiked up his pants and pressed a button on the side of the robot. The DeliveryBot sprung to life, its tracks whirring as it prepared to unload the crate.

The driver glanced at his screen. "Says here it came from Chicago."

Hearing "Chicago" made me freeze for a moment.

"What do you think it is?" Kieran asked, joining me at the bottom of the steps.

"I'm not sure," I replied, my mind already swirling with possibilities.

The driver, looking impatient, asked, "So, where do you want it?"

I gestured toward the red-and-white barn, freshly painted by Tellman's nephew, who was trying to save up for a Hover ATV. "In the barn, next to the Nutrient Analyzer should work."

The DeliveryBot moved like a mechanical forklift, lifting the massive crate with ease and rolling it down the ramp. Kieran ran ahead to swing open the barn doors, excitement clear in his steps.

"Did it come with any paperwork?" I asked as I followed behind.

"There was a note, actually. Handwritten. Isn't that nuts? Most folks don't bother with paper anymore." The driver pulled a crumpled envelope from his back pocket, bent and dirt-smudged.

"Thanks." I took it and watched as Kieran directed the DeliveryBot to place the crate in just the right spot. Curiosity gnawed at me as I opened the envelope and read the note inside.

I thought you'd want her back. Some things are worth rebuilding, especially with a little help. — K.

A strange rush of emotion hit me—excitement, wonder. I glanced toward the crate and Kieran, and a smile spread across my face.

"I think we've got it from here," I told the driver, waving him off. "You can call your robot back."

"He can help you unbox it if you want," the driver called over his shoulder.

"I don't think we'll need any help." My grin widened as I approached the crate.

The DeliveryBot paused, as if waiting for confirmation, but then it rolled back toward the truck, leaving us alone with the mystery box.

Kieran was already trying to pry the boards off with his bare hands. Though strong, he needed the right tool. I fetched a crowbar from the tool rack and handed it to him. "Here, try this."

Kieran took it eagerly and set to work. "What do you think is in here?"

"A gift from Katrina," I said, my voice tinged with something between disbelief and hope.

"Katrina?" He wedged the crowbar into the crate and pried off the boards with a satisfying crack. After a few moments of searching, his hand found a smooth, silver object nestled in protective foam. Gently, he pulled it out and held it up for me to see—a delicate faceplate with intricate features. Aria's face. The soft curves of her cheekbones, the shape of her eyes, all instantly recognizable. "She used to smile like this," Kieran said, tracing his fingers along the edges, his voice almost reverent. "Don't worry, Uncle Eli. I know exactly how to fix her."

We spent the rest of the afternoon unpacking the pieces of Aria. Somehow, Katrina—or perhaps Dr. Liu—had managed to salvage her from the robot meltdown. Someday, maybe, I'd ask them how they did it. But for now, we had work to do. As we gathered all the pieces, Kieran began explaining how, with his mother's files and knowledge, he could rebuild Aria and make her better than before.

As I looked out toward the mountains framed in the open barn door, I realized soon Aria would finally see the world Meredith and I had loved. For the first time, she'd feel the sun on the ranch, hear the wind in the trees, and stand where Meredith once stood. And in those moments, I'd be living it all again—through her eyes, and the memory of the woman who made her.

The End

ABOUT THE AUTHOR

K. J. Gillenwater worked as a Russian linguist in the U.S. Navy, spending time at the National Security Agency doing secret things. After six years of service, she ended up as a technical writer in the software industry. She has lived all over the U.S. and currently resides in Wyoming with her family, writing government proposals and crafting captivating fiction on her days off. She likes her dogs, sunrises, and car radio karaoke.

Visit K.J.'s website for more information about her writing, her books, and what's coming next. www.kjgillenwater.com.

If you enjoyed this book, K. J. Gillenwater is the author of multiple books, which are available in print and in eBook format.

Full-length Books:

- The Automated Series: System Override, Rebellion Protocol
- The Genesis Machine Trilogy: Inception, Decryption, and Revelation
- The Aurora Series: Aurora's Gold and Aurora's Winter
- Revenge Honeymoon
- Illegal
- The Ninth Curse

- The Little Black Box
- Acapulco Nights
- Blood Moon

Short Stories & Short Story Collections:

- Skyfall
- Nemesis
- The Man in 14C
- Charlie and the Zombie Factory

Audiobooks (Audible):

- The Genesis Machine Trilogy: Inception,
  Decryption, and Revelation